BROTHER OF MINE

CHRIS · WESTWOOD

BROTHER OF MINE

CLARION BOOKS · NEW YORK

Clarion Books
a Houghton Mifflin Company imprint
215 Park Avenue South, New York, NY 10003
Text copyright © 1994 by Chris Westwood

Previously published in England by Viking Kestrel, 1993.
Type is New Baskerville and Futura Book

Printed in the USA

Library of Congress Cataloging-in-Publication Data

Westwood, Chris.
Brother of mine / by Chris Westwood.
p.   cm.
Summary: Sixteen-year-old twins, Nick and Tony, always envious of
each other's talents, reveal, in alternate chapters, their differing
perspectives of their sometimes complicated relationship.
ISBN 0-395-66137-4
[1. Sibling rivalry—Fiction.   2. Brothers—Fiction.   3. Twins—
Fiction.   4. Identity—Fiction.]   I. Title.
PZ7.W5274Br   1994
[Fic]—dc20   92-32020
                                                      CIP
                                                      AC

BP   10   9   8   7   6   5   4   3   2   1

BROTHER OF MINE

1 NICK

*I*n the dream, it is always the same. Our mother is on the main street, shoulders drooping with shopping, when she feels the first kick inside.

She gasps, as if an idea has just struck her: an idea that will change the world. She stops in the doorway outside Woolworth, puts her bags at her feet, fingers her belly, which bulges inside her maternity smock; and a faint smile meets her lips. Shoppers come and go, blurry and faceless. It comes again, a jolt like a small, dull electric charge. Her fingers tap away at her belly as she murmurs, "There now, there now, that's enough of that. . . ." She waits a long moment before deciding she's able to move on.

Inside our mother, I am almost completely formed. In spite of the dark and the unsteady rhythm of her heart that sometimes makes it hard for me to relax or think or sleep, I can tell I have fingers, five on each hand including thumbs, and that toes have developed at the tips of my feet. I'm suspended in space like a satellite, knees jarring into my chest for lack of anywhere else to put them. It isn't an ideal arrangement, but it's home. Our mother's voice—she spends so much time talking to her belly, prodding it, slapping, considering it—this is a part of life too, so much a part it's hard to imagine being without it.

What I could live without, though, is Tony—Tony the Other, as I've come to see him. I wake and there he is, staring, watching me, not letting me settle for a second. Sometimes I'm afraid to sleep: Who knows what he'll be up to the minute my back is turned? When he sees me staring back, he will speak.

"When the time comes," he says, "I'm going first."

Or, with the same indignant delivery:

"Move over, you're eating up my space."

Worse still, one bad morning or night after our mother has been sick for so long that everything in our world seems to shiver and quake:

"Who do you think you are? *I* was here first."

This is how it is, how we grow, in an atmosphere of fear and rivalry that no loving words or drumming fingers can soothe. At times Tony becomes purely physical. He runs out of arguments and kicks out. Our mother jumps: On the main street she drops both bags.

What she doesn't understand is that it's *me* he's lashing out at, not her. It's me he wants to hurt. Each time her voice begins again, coaxing, small-talking, he glares at me as if it's intended for his ears only. He kicks out once more, and I recoil.

"Remember," he says, "who she's talking to."

Then, one day, or night, which all come alike in this

endlessly dark place, I open my eyes and blink disbelievingly. We are either too large—we have grown con-
siderably since that time on the main street—or our
mother's abdomen is shrinking. Tony seems to be trying
to stand, to inflate himself, make himself larger than
me. I have this vague sense of the walls closing in all
around us, the way they do in nightmare sequences in
films. The even thunder of our mother's heartbeat has
become something more: an uncontrolled sprint, the
rhythm of a speeding train as it enters a tunnel where
the sound becomes suddenly amplified and trapped,
more and more urgent. Our mother is in pain. She
doesn't even think to speak to us now.

Tony stares at me, triumphant.

"I'm getting out of here," he tells me. "Don't you dare
follow."

"What else can I do? We've always done everything
together."

"Just stay here. Don't move and don't try to follow.
Otherwise—you'll get what you deserve."

My God, I think. He wants it *all.*

All at once, I've had enough—these nine solid months
of repression have finally made a revolutionary of me,
and I snap. Tony is forcing himself away from me, crossing into deeper and deeper darkness, entering a place
from which there's no turning back. Somehow I always
knew we were heading that way, but I never imagined
it would happen so soon.

Suddenly I feel afraid. Tony will take his leave and
seal up the exit after him, I know he will, he'll do anything to keep whatever comes next for himself. It isn't
that he wants to be the first but the *only.* Whatever we

have in common he wants to deny. Perhaps it is fear, or anger at Tony, but as he vanishes into the blackness, I fling myself after him, seizing his legs.

Tony tries to resist. "Get off me, get out of my *face!*"

He flails at me, both legs at once, hauls himself forward as best he can. His voice sounds mute and far away.

"You're too late, Nick, too late. . . ."

The next thing I know, our mother is gasping and heaving, choking out words I can't understand—and there are other voices, many voices.

My wrestling match with Tony is the thing that hurts her the most. I let go, and his feet pass, slippery, between my fully formed fingers. I can feel his body lurch some distance ahead of me in the tunnel, and instinctively I throw myself backward to avoid being kicked one last time before he joins our mother outside.

Then, for the first time ever, I am alone.

I stay huddled where I am, barely suspended in moisture and space, knowing that sooner or later I'll have to follow. Deep down I know our mother knows about me too; that it isn't only Tony she wants. It's only the thought of Tony—what he might do if I dare to follow—that holds me back.

There is pressure from above me, a hand pressing down, and more voices I don't recognize, and again the sensation of walls closing in. Far away I hear a slap, a yell, my brother making noises for attention. The hand presses down again, and I turn. It looks as though this is it, whether I want to go or not. In the end I don't have a choice.

In the dream, it is always the same.

2 TONY

First thing Thursday morning, and I'm scarcely through the school gates when this friend of mine, Keith Dent—who's this thick-set, shaggy-haired, rugby-playing outdoors type who you really wouldn't want to mess with, and who I've known for as long as I can remember, since before I started at Milton Green High—comes charging toward me out of nowhere. Before I've had time to figure what's happening, he's seized hold of my school tie and practically raised me off the ground, choking me. His teeth are gritted and bared in anger; his right hand is a clenched fist poised ready to strike. The last time I saw Keith, apart from at school, we were at his place two nights ago playing poker and pool, joking about and having kicks. And now this.

"Apologize," he says—sort of seethes—through his teeth. "Apologize now, or I swear to God I'll do something we'll both regret later."

"Keith! What's this about? No, don't hit me! What am I supposed to apologize *for*?"

"You know well enough," he says, slightly relaxing his grip. He lowers and unclenches his fist. "It's just a good thing I've had time to calm down, that's all."

"You don't look so calm. What's the problem?"

"Everything you said on the phone, that's what. What the hell do you *think* is the problem?" He's glaring at me as if we're archenemies, as if we've never been friends or gone camping together or played in that band Keith was the singer in or anything. "Do you need me to refresh your memory?"

"You'd better."

"You're kidding. You must have some nerve, Tony. Not only do you insult me, but now you pretend you know nothing about it."

"Insult you?" I'm stunned, almost speechless. "Keith, you're my friend. When did I ever insult you?"

"Spare me." He rolls his eyes heavenward, and when he looks back at me, his anger seems to be rising again. "Last night when I phoned to say I couldn't meet you in town and you acted hurt and disappointed. And then you got abusive and . . . Why am I telling you this? You were there."

"But I wasn't," I tell him, plead with him. "I'd left a message to say *I* couldn't make it. I was over at Vicky's until late."

There's a pause. In his eyes, blue murder gives way to confusion. "You—you weren't *there*? Then what—then who was I talking to?"

Which is when the twisted truth about what must have

happened hits both of us. We look at each other for a long, awkward moment, and then Keith lets go of my tie and we both turn to stare across the yard. In the middle distance there's Vicky, walking toward us slowly and nervously, as if she's treading on eggshells, aware that there's something bad in the air. Beyond her, near the main entrance where the locker rooms are, her girl friends stand watching like gossip-hungry vultures. And then I see Nick and the pack of dropouts he calls friends, Terry Mulligan, Bob Clark, a few others. They too are watching, and though we can't see their faces from where we're standing, we can sense the smirks, the atmosphere of amusement, as though they're all sharing the same telepathic laugh-in party line.

"Hey, boys. What's up?" Vicky says when she reaches us. Her mousy hair is tied back in a braid this morning, and her dark eyes are cautious. She touches my arm gently and puts on a face. "Can't you be bothered to come say good morning?"

"I didn't have the chance yet," I tell her, and Keith says, "So this message you left for me, Tony. Who did you leave it *with*?"

"I left it by the phone, so that anyone who answered would see it if you rang."

"What's the problem?" Vicky asks, exasperated. "What's going on between you two?"

"Nick is the problem," Keith says bluntly.

"He's been pretending to be me on the phone again," I add. A jet passes loudly overhead, drowning out the screams and chants of the kids in the yards for a minute. The noise falls over us like dust.

"Again?" Keith's eyes widen. "You mean he does this kind of thing for kicks?"

"I can't imagine what he gets out of it, but this isn't the first time by any means."

Vicky shakes her head stiffly. "That's odd." The bell is going for homeroom, and we begin walking toward the school building. "Have you ever asked him why he was doing it?" she says.

"Once, but he pleaded ignorance. In fact, he didn't pay much attention at all when I brought it up. In the end I let the thing drop."

"Maybe it's just a phase he's going through," Vicky offers. "Have you done anything to upset him lately?"

I shrug, put my hands in my pockets. Ahead of us the last of the uniformed mob is disappearing inside the entrance, Nick and his cronies among them. As we head indoors through the locker rooms toward the corridor that smells like a hospital, Keith stops by the door to the boys' toilet and says, "Tony, listen, I'm sorry about the misunderstanding, really I am. It just never entered my head that I wasn't speaking to you. He *sounded* like you, every bit like you. He *said* he was you." As an afterthought he adds, "*I* should give him something to be upset about." Then he hammers open the door fit to bust the hinges and steps inside.

"All this aggression," Vicky goes, shaking her head. "Maybe what Nick needs is a little goodwill, less of these threats and promises. Maybe if you sat down and talked things out."

"Sure," I go, hardly listening. But I'm thinking: What he needs is a damn good hiding. What in the world is *wrong* with him anyway? Why is he doing this, trying to ruin things between me and my friends?

At the end of the first stretch of gray-tiled corridor, we turn right into another. Three doors along on the right stands Nick, the rest of the class having filed inside D3. As we come nearer, Nick beams and puts out his hand.

"Tony! Vicky! How's everything?"

Which is when I take him and slam him against the wall.

3 <u>NICK</u>

You should see his face; it's that look that comes over him in the dream. One of these days, I tell myself, the kid's going to lose complete control. Just for a second his eyes are kind of blazing and dark and his lips are quivering.

Then he lets me go and backs off, dusting his blazer, straightening his tie.

"What was *that* for?" I go.

"You know," he says.

He lets Vicky Riley slide past me, then follows her inside D3. I stand there a minute longer, straightening my own tie. As I'm doing this, I see Mr. Rees come lurching along the corridor with that wheeling, long-striding way he has, like some slob of a sergeant about to inspect the enlisted men's quarters. He coughs to remind me I'm loitering, and I step inside the class. Paper planes fill the air, pens and pencils fly back and forth like missiles, and there's a gradually building chorus of chaos that never quite reaches its peak before Rees makes the door and thirty-two bottoms hit their seats as one.

My desk is directly behind Tony's, and I'm sitting staring at the space between his shoulders when he wheels around as if he can't keep this in any longer and hisses at me, "You nearly screwed me up this time. What do you think you're doing?"

"Huh?" I play dumb; at the moment I don't know what else to do. As if it isn't enough to threaten me with violence, he's now trying to suggest he has good reason.

"Tony," I say, and show him my palms. "Whatever it is I'm supposed to have done—I mean, if this has anything to do with Keith, it was all a joke. Really, I never meant any harm—"

"Nicholas *Lloyd!*" This is Rees's voice, hard and direct as a swinging fist, and it isn't that he's calling my name from the register. He adds quietly, "Since you obviously have so much to talk about, you won't mind finishing your discussion after school. With me."

By the time Rees has finished passing sentence, Tony is seated innocently facing the front, arms folded, as if what has just happened doesn't concern him. This isn't the first time he's drawn me in like this; it's always been his knack to get off lightly, leaving me to face the consequences. Even his name, which comes right before mine on the register, is treated lightly by Rees: Anthony Lloyd = sunlight on water, blackbirds singing at dusk. And then Rees calls my name, which sounds like bile behind his clenched teeth.

What's happening to us? I sometimes wonder. Why

is he doing this to me? This morning I woke with the sun in my eyes, feeling ready to leap up and seize the day. All I could think of was the interschool sports meet on the weekend, for which I'm in training for the 800 and 1500 meters, and legging the two and a quarter miles to Milton Green instead of taking the school bus with Tony. Perhaps, if I timed it right, I could be there before him—not much of a challenge, considering the slovenly bus service between here and there—but the thrill would be feeling the wind in my face, enduring the long and arduous up-curving main road from Forest Hill before the steep downgrade to Milton, and that sudden soaring: Yes, I made it, I'm *home*. . . .

So after mentally replaying this several times, I'm bustling about, not a thought in my head except where are my Nikes and what books do I need for school, all the while with this picture in my mind of the athletic field painted up for the track events and the finish-line tape stretching across the eight lanes, rushing nearer and nearer as I accelerate. I hardly register Tony sitting at the table eating breakfast, and pause only to lift a slice of buttered toast from his plate on my way out the door. He scowls but doesn't speak.

"See you later," I say, and our mother shouts something after me that I pretend not to hear. If I turn back and ask her to repeat it, I know I'll lose momentum, so instead I announce loudly when I expect to be home and dodge out the front door.

Of the two and a quarter miles between home and school, at least the first half is a gentle uphill climb before you reach Forest Hill, where Vicky Riley lives in a town house facing the main road where it begins to rise more sharply. Vicky is just leaving as I pass her gate, and I wonder briefly if I should stop and say hello and risk being overtaken by the bus. She looks pretty and fresh faced, her hair tied back in a pigtail or braid. Instead I just wave, slowing only to switch my school bag, heavy with books, and the black polished brogues that go with my uniform, from right to left shoulder.

"Hey, Tony!" she shouts, then immediately realizes her mistake. She's been seeing him for months and still can't tell us apart at a distance. "Hey, Nick, how are you?"

I'm on top of the world by the time I make the yard at Milton Green High. I'm there in good time, I'm ready to take on all comers on the weekend—even Billy Mayhew from Calderwood School. I'm hardly even perspiring, and if I half close my eyes, I can practically see the finish-line tape rushing toward me. And when Tony whacks me against the wall and then Rees gives me this damn detention, it's as if that world has just slipped away from under me. Even after the bell goes to end homeroom, and then half an hour later morning assembly, and then later still art with Miss Welles, you can tell he's still seething at me over nothing.

Miss Welles is a sweet young twentyish redheaded woman not wearing a wedding ring (I notice these things) and with a low, husky voice that reminds me of someone I saw in an old black-and-white film once. She is leaning across my desk taking in the pencil sketch I've been working on. I'm almost embarrassingly aware of her next to me, the smell of her talc mingling with the

fixative and linseed oil in the air. The sketch is a preliminary for a painting I'd like to move on to later. In it a
young man gazes into an oval mirror, in which his reflection smiles broadly back at him. The thing is, the
man himself isn't smiling at all; only his reflection is
smiling.

Miss Welles says, "Mmm. Very interesting." But I
don't hold the dumb comment against her. "Where did
you get the idea?" she asks.

Which is when the bell goes, and before I can find
time to answer, she loses interest and stands up, claps
her hands, tells the class, "See you all tomorrow, then."

Past her I see Tony, rising to his feet so slowly it's
easy to believe he's running on drained batteries. While
he packs up his stuff, he's staring at me without expression. By the time I've packed up my own belongings,
we're practically the only two left in the room.

"One of these days I'll swing for you," he goes.

"Sure," I go, humoring him—but at heart I know
what he really means, and I don't feel as untroubled as
I make myself sound.

4 <u>TONY</u>

How things came to be the way they are between him and me, I couldn't even hazard a guess. But if we're going to dig deep into it, then it's probably worth mentioning how we grew up—through the early years, at least. That was when our folks were still struggling and the house was a two-up two-down row house in a dowdy part of Wakefield sandwiched between the prison and a bread factory. For too many years Nick and I shared the same room, and my clearest memory of that time involves being woken by him, not by his snoring but his silence.

It was sometime after midnight one night. All at once I was wide awake, probably because our curtains hadn't closed out the moon, which was shining straight in my eyes. At first I just sort of lay there, waiting for sleep to come again, and then gradually I sensed Nick watching from his bed across the room.

He was sitting bolt upright, straight-backed, staring

intently. For a while I feigned sleep, at the same time watching *him* through half-closed eyes. He never moved. Once he folded his arms across his chest, then unfolded them again and sat on his hands. In the dark, especially through half-closed eyes, I couldn't make out his features or be sure what was happening, but I do remember the way his head was cocked to one side like a dog's.

In the end I couldn't fake it any longer. "Nick?" I yawned.

"Sshh. Get back to sleep. Don't worry about me."

"I'm not."

A year or so later I caught him again—on a similar bright night, in the same fixed pose, cross-legged on his bed.

"Just watching you sleep," he told me this time. "Can't sleep myself, so I'm watching you instead."

I wasn't sure I liked the idea of that—it made me feel spied on—and until we moved eighteen months later, my nights were restless, my schoolwork was suffering. Twice in the same week I overslept, nearly missing morning homeroom. Both times I arrived in class breathless and sweating like a hog—Nick is the long-distance runner, not me—to find him smiling secretly as if he'd planned the whole thing.

Then our folks found a house they liked and could just about afford in St. Dominic's Grove, near Forest Hill, an old stone house on the edge of a new development with much more space outside and in. Out the back there was a patio and a long, untended lawn that my dad said he'd soon hack into shape for the summer (we moved in one March), and indoors was a kitchen that answered our mother's prayers and an extra room upstairs that answered mine. At this point I didn't care which I took, and when Nick made a play for the larger room, I let him have it without fuss.

It was after we went our separate ways, at least as far as sleeping was concerned, that I began to notice other things about Nick. Maybe they'd been obvious all along and I'd been too close or too tired from interrupted sleep to see.

"What other things?" Vicky Riley asks as we head home from school on Thursday. We're walking hand in hand, which is what she seems to want and expect, though her friends—Pam and Tracy and Stacey—are trailing only twenty or thirty yards behind us, whistling and catcalling now and again. The girls she hangs out with you wouldn't believe—seven-year-olds from the neck up—but Vicky herself is wiser and you'd almost think older, and looks smart and sharp in her school uniform. Nick had a thing for her once, about a year ago almost, and sometimes I wonder whether *that's* his real problem, the fact that she chose me over him. But I'm drifting, daydreaming, and Vicky is saying, "What *kind* of other things? What else did you notice about him?"

"Well, at one time—that time—our mother used to dress us both exactly the same even apart from school. God knows why she did, but more often than not you'd find us dressed up on weekends in identical everythings down to the socks and shoes."

"Maybe she just liked the idea of your being identical," Vicky suggests. "She was proud of her twins."

"She *loved* the idea, but she never knew when to stop, was all. For instance: If one of us ragged up a new pair of jeans or scuffed up our shoes, she'd buy replacements for *both* of us; she didn't think of us as separate at all. Still doesn't." I let this sink home for a minute before continuing. "One thing she did once that struck me as especially wacky was when she had these little identification pins with our names on made up so that people who didn't know us could tell us apart—most relatives and neighbors just couldn't."

"Even *I* have to get up close," Vicky says with a meaningful laugh.

"She had our names stitched on our jackets and sweaters: Nicholas and Anthony, as she liked to call us then. She'd introduce us to people who would look at our clothes first, our faces second. Still gives me the jitters to think about it." We walk in silence for a while up the slope toward Forest Hill. It's warm and dry, and I loosen my tie as we go, then pull it off altogether and stuff it deep down in a pocket. Then I say, "What Nick used to do was switch our clothing. If he went out without me, he'd whip my jacket off the peg and leave me with his. And sometimes I'd find his clothes—only the ones with the name sewn on—in my drawer, in my room. And mine in his. It was like he'd be walking around in my stuff and I'd be expected to walk around in his."

"What was he trying to prove?" Vicky asks.

I can only shrug. "When I asked him about it, he just sniffed and said, 'Sorry, my mistake.' Except that I knew it wasn't a mistake."

She's shivering now, although the mid-June afternoon is arid, the air heavy with pollens. On the way up the hill we pass a garden exploding with white and yellow roses, and the scent makes me sneeze loudly and violently. Behind us Vicky's girl friends titter among themselves, and I turn to scowl after them.

"I never imagined it was like that between you," Vicky says.

"It was *then*," I tell her. "These days it's different. He plays other games now, like the one with Keith Dent. He's even picked up on things that I say, certain phrases, and sometimes he'll mimic my voice."

"Is he . . ." She firms her hold on my hand. "Does he have something against you? Has he ever tried to hurt you?"

I shrug but don't answer. We're almost at her gateway now, so we stop for a minute and stare at each other. Her cheeks are dimpled, her skin very clear and faintly dusted with freckles. She has lived with her folks here in Forest Hill all her life, and sometimes it gives me a strange kind of thrill to think back to the days before we moved and changed schools when I didn't know Vicky existed. We're still standing saying nothing when her friends catch up to us, leering as they pass like some three-headed monster with a warped sense of humor, then bursting into laughter ten or twelve yards farther on.

"One of these days," I say through clenched teeth.

"Never mind. Would you like to come in for coffee?" she asks.

In the kitchen, which faces south and is filled with yellow light at this hour, she hands me a towel so I can wipe the sweat from my palms while I sit at the table. Everything in Vicky's kitchen is designer stripped pine and so clean it's hard to imagine anyone actually cooking in here. Vicky brings two steaming mugs to the table, sets them down, then unexpectedly sits on my lap.

"Anything else you'd like?" she says, then laughs freely. "I meant *apart* from that."

We kiss on and off for a while, though she won't let me do anything with my hands. "Dream on," she says, and eases around to the next stripped-pine dining chair, where she lolls, flushed and smiling. "My mom and dad will be home before long."

"Do they both get off work early today?"

"Early enough to keep you in your place, my man."

I make a face and she makes one back. We both laugh spontaneously. Then I slurp my coffee, so noisily she throws a cork coaster at my head. Suddenly, though, her mood shifts and she's staring into her mug as if searching for a solution to some puzzle or other.

"Sometimes I feel sorry for him," she admits. "Nick, I mean. Sometimes I wonder whether . . ."

"What?"

"Never mind. It's nothing."

"No," I insist. "You were about to say something. Sometimes you wonder . . . ?"

She takes her time, measuring her words with care. "Whether he feels the same way about you as you do about him. He looked so taken aback today when you grabbed him, so defenseless."

"Meaning what?"

"I said it was nothing, Tony."

But it's more than nothing to her, I can tell. Slightly flustered, I fold up the towel and slap it down and run my fingers through my hair to rough it up.

"Really," she says. "All I'm saying is that maybe there are two sides to every story, and if Nick behaves strangely, he could have his reasons, couldn't he?"

"What reasons?"

"Why are you doing this?" she replies, looking rattled and anxious. "First you paint this very black picture of your brother, and then you hit out at me just because I wonder how it looks from his side."

"I'm not hitting out. Or even painting him black. Don't you believe what I told you?"

"Oh, shut up." She gets up from the table and pours her undrunk coffee down the sink, where she stands looking out through the window at nothing. The sky over Forest Hill is more golden than blue. "You'd better go now," she says.

"What are we arguing about?" I ask.

"Nothing at all. This is so damn silly."

"I agree. You still want me to go?"

"My mom and dad will be home before long," she repeats.

"I'm sorry," I say, and plant a dry kiss on the back of her neck before leaving. "I'm sorry for carrying on." She is still staring outdoors when I turn from the kitchen. Then she scurries after me, seeing me out. At the front door she stands watching me, gnawing her lip. I touch her cheek and she relaxes a little.

"Don't worry," I tell her. "It's something and nothing. I'll call you from home later on."

But Vicky is nonetheless worried. "Where do they come from, these moments? Why are we so silly?"

"God knows, but we are. Still friends?"

"Still friends."

At the gate when I turn to look back, she waves and blows a kiss before slipping indoors. So it's over and there's nothing to worry about. It's our first real tiff, which is probably the only bothersome thing about it.

By the time I'm at home, though, hanging up my tie and loosening my shoelaces, I'm niggled by the idea she'd want to see anything from *his* point of view. After a while I pick up my guitar, which I used to play in this band I formed with Keith Dent called POV, and bash out a few chords, trying to push everything out of my mind. Nick and Vicky, Vicky and me . . . It isn't that I'm jealous, even if every story does have two sides. It's more that I wouldn't want to feel he could influence her against me for any reason, make her believe all kinds of lies about me.

5 <u>NICK</u>

*I*n the backseat of Terry Mulligan's older brother's car, there are two others beside me, and we're packed so tight, I can't even free my arm to roll down the window to breathe. Terry is up front in the passenger seat, and his brother, Phil, is at the wheel. After we've driven around for a while—we don't seem to be going any-where in particular—Phil twists around to me and says, "Are you sure you want to come along with us? Isn't it past your *bed*time?"

"I'm good for a few hours yet," I tell him.

The others in the back with me (I don't know and don't care who they are, but they're nearer Phil's age, eighteen) sniff and snicker. Terry leans forward to fid-dle with the radio, though the only sound it produces is crackling static.

"Must get an antenna for this thing," Phil says.

As far as I can tell we're still in Milton, in the shopping streets about a mile beyond the school. It's that time of night when the gangs are roaming, many of them juniors and seniors, all dressed up with nowhere worthwhile to go to. Many are moving from pub to pub; others haunt bus depots, street corners, people watching. The girls are in short skirts and shorts this summer, and their faces are daubed with mascara and blusher. The boys are in shirtsleeves and stonewashed denims, and some of them still have on sunglasses. From where I'm sitting they all look alike, but why they would want to look alike defeats me.

"There's Gary," says Terry suddenly, slapping the window on his side. "Is there room for one more in the back?"

"Sure," I go, but the others beside me groan. One of them lights up a cigarette, and the smoke makes my eyes smart at once.

"Well?" Terry says. "Do you or don't you want to know where it is?"

"All right," Phil says, and pulls over.

As soon as Gary is wedged in the back, half on and half off my lap, he says, short of breath, "It's in the Rosemount development, where those old stone houses are being renovated. There's a whole row down near the fields that's still empty."

"How'd you find out about this?" Terry asks.

"Bob Clark's dad was the foreman of the builders that refurbished the row. Bob got a copy of the house key somehow."

"That villain," Phil marvels. "At his age he ought to know better."

"And does everything work there?" goes Terry. "Is

everything connected? Electricity, I mean, for the sounds?"

"No," Gary says, sort of sarcastically. "The idea is for everyone to sit around in silence in the dark doing nothing. That's this year's thing, don't you know."

"Smart mouth," says Terry, and everyone laughs—except Gary and myself: I'm too squashed to find anything funny.

Before long we're leaving the shopping center behind and idling through the quiet Rosemount development. At the upper end, nearer town, the houses are of the modern semidetached kind with communal lawns, no fences or private gardens, built probably within the last two or three years. The street names are as bland as the properties look: Wilmsley Crescent, Wilton Way, Allum Road, Alcott Grove. It strikes me how easy it would be to get lost in this maze. If you ever run away from home and don't want to be found, this is your place.

Farther along the houselights peter out and the streetlights pick out For Sale signs, one after another. Phil slows the car and rolls down his window, and though I'd like to do the same, my arm is crushed and numb, immobile. These are the older, stone-fronted houses Gary mentioned. There are perhaps twelve of them, six either side of the narrow road. Past them, the headlights flare and solid ground seems to disappear altogether, as if we're veering toward a cliff edge.

"There's the fields," Terry says.

We're close to the place we're looking for. There's a handful of cars parked near this end of the road. I'm almost sure I hear music somewhere, the beat rather than the melody, and then we're drawing up outside a house where the windows are lit and inside looks busy with movement. Whoever they are, they're here in numbers.

There's a cement mixer on the drive outside that the workmen have left, and as we spill from the car (the right side of my body is paralyzed now) one of Phil's friends says, "I know someone who could use a thing like that."

Yourself, to unmix your *brain*, I think, following the others up to the house. After a minute Bob Clark comes to the door and a big cheer goes up before he lets us inside. I'm still wondering what I'm doing here when someone else I don't know jams a can of warm beer into my hand. Incredibly I can't think of any sane reason except that I didn't feel ready to head home and face Tony in case he hadn't cooled down yet. But if anyone ought to feel grieved, it's me: After all, where was *he* when I was in detention with Rees?

"Why can't you follow your brother's example?" Rees said before sending me home—nearer five than four-thirty, the sadist. "Then you wouldn't have to face me."

"I'll bear that in mind, sir," I said as I packed up my stuff and changed into my sneakers again. Taking my chances, I left my shoes and books in an empty unused locker in the locker room and ran over to Terry Mulligan's instead of home.

For a while at the party I just wander from room to empty room. The floors are still uncovered bare concrete smeared with plaster dust and cement, but it's easy to see why someone would want to live here. The ceilings are high, and many walls are wood paneled, while the doors are solid and oaky and the fittings have a built-to-last feel. It may be an old place, but I'd rather have this than the cardboard boxes farther up the development. In one of the rooms someone has set up two CD players, one for the music which is hammering out through two Wharfedale speakers hooked up to a Kenwood amp, and another that's displaying colored kaleidoscopic patterns on a large TV in a corner. Very few of the kids in the room are dancing, preferring instead to watch and wait; almost all are older than me—as if the fact I haven't changed out of my uniform isn't bad enough. Flustered by the way they're staring at me, I strip off my tie and pocket it, then take a sip from the can and lean against the door, nodding my head to the bass riff.

The beer tastes as if someone peed in it, so I set it down on the floor and walk away from it. In another room—the kitchen—Bob and Phil and Phil's two Neanderthal friends are talking cars and motorbikes, so I stand listening for a while, trying to seem interested. Then I notice, across the kitchen, a large dark door that doesn't quite blend in with the overall look of the house. The workmen can't have dealt with it yet. There's a rusted and rickety lock with a key in it.

What's in there? I wonder, but no one hears me, so I move to the door and unlock it. Both the key and the door handle are stiff and need coaxing, and the hinges grate as I push the door open. The next thing I know,

I'm peering down into darkness—what I've found is the cellar—and almost at once I hear something moving below me.

At first I imagine what I've heard is an animal, since the sound is so small and slight. Then someone gasps out, "Thank goodness. Could you put on the light, please? It's inside the door on the right."

It takes me a second to find and fumble it on. After that I have a view of the cellar below me, the stone steps leading down and empty sacks and crates of newspapers that have been dumped at the bottom. Standing near the middle of the floor, looking up, shielding her eyes against the sudden surge of electric light, is a girl with dark but white-dusted hair wearing black dungarees, which I notice are torn at the knees. She sighs and makes a move for the steps.

"Thank you. I was beginning to get desperate."

"What happened?" I ask. "What are you doing down there in the dark?"

"You wouldn't believe me if I told you," she says. You can tell how strained her face is even before she steps into the better light in the kitchen. The others sort of sniff and grin when they set eyes on her, but otherwise ignore us, continuing their discussion of crankshafts and clutch plates. "Nobody noticed I was down there, exploring. I'd only left the party for a minute and—well, suddenly the light goes off and the door slams shut and I hear it lock above me. Didn't anyone hear me calling?"

"Didn't anyone hear her calling?" I ask, and Phil and Bob shrug while the bonehead brothers don't react at all.

She dusts herself down and shakes her head, rattled.

"Are you all right?" I ask, indicating her torn dungarees. Her exposed knees are scraped and bloody. "Can I help?"

"Oh, this? Don't worry. That was me being a klutz, trying to find my way up the steps in the dark. The price you pay for prying. Thanks again for everything. I suppose I'd better get back to the party now."

"Are you here with someone?" I go, sounding slightly more anxious than I mean to. "That is, will someone have noticed you missing?"

She looks at me for a long moment, during which I can feel myself flush. Perhaps noticing, she tosses her head back and smiles very faintly with small and perfectly formed teeth. "Just my cousin," she says finally. "Neil Templeton. Maybe you know him?"

"No, don't think so."

"But you go to Milton Green High?"

"Afraid so."

"Maybe it isn't as bad as all that." She pauses. "I'm staying with Neil and his family." Then she lowers her voice confidentially. "If I'd known this was the kind of place he meant to bring me, I wouldn't have come."

"Then you would've missed all the fun," I say.

"Sure, the grimy cellar, the spiders, the dark. And to think I could've been in Florida instead."

"You're kidding."

"Not at all. Thing being, my parents are separated, and it was a case of either come here or go with my mother to *her* mother's in Liverpool, or stay with my dad and his floozie in Florida. But I can't *stand* the floo-

zie and I haven't quite forgiven him for leaving, so—"
She stops herself there, openmouthed. "What am I telling you for? You don't want to hear this."

"I don't mind if you don't," I tell her.

She puts out her hand and we shake like business associates, but suddenly this feels to me more like pleasure than business. With her scuffed knees and dusty hair, there's something so natural, so unforced about her, I want to ask aloud what the secret is.

"Alex," she says, and after a lull I say, "Nick. Nick Lloyd."

Together we move through to the room where the music is, but loiter near the door where the sound and smoke are less penetrating. Across the room a senior I know only by sight, whose long lank blond hair falls over one eye, gazes up from the CD display, waving when he sees us. I'm about to wave back, not knowing why, when Alex shouts in my ear, "That's my cousin Neil. Now that he's seen me, he'll forget about me for another two hours."

"Isn't he supposed to be looking after you?"

"He thinks I'm too old to need looking after and not old enough to be seen with," she shouts. Then, "Are you sure *you* don't mind being seen with me?"

"I guess I'll be able to live it down."

With a forefinger she presses my nose like a button. "You know, you're all right. You have my approval."

And though I'd like to answer her wittily, I only smile. Let me tell you, my nerves are beginning to flutter at this point. Not that I'm afraid of Alex, just of behaving clumsily or saying the wrong thing until I know her.

Tony has always been the one with a knack for girls—
and although that's something of a sore point with me,
I find myself wishing I could be more like him while
I'm with her.

After a while she leads me outside the back way,
through the kitchen, where Bob and Phil's group are
still talking, and we stand in a dark, sweet-smelling
garden that lies mostly in shadow despite the crescent
moon above the fields. "It's all overgrown," she says.
"But imagine what it could be like with a little love
and attention. What can you smell?—Roses? Orange
blossoms?"

"Mmm," I go, though I wouldn't know one from the
other. In the darkness a moth strikes my forehead and
I waft it away.

"Lavender too," she goes on. "Where I live with my
mother, there's nothing but houses, and concrete yards.
The only plants there come in tubs."

"How long are you here for?" I ask after an interval.

"Two or three weeks." She turns to me. "But it's flex-
ible. Could be longer if I decide it's worth staying."

"Can I—" I begin, but my mouth is suddenly bone
dry, and I'm forced to clear my throat to avoid a
coughing fit. "Will I see you again while you're here?"

"If you'd like."

It's really as simple as that. For a moment or two I
just stand there, overawed, after which I relax and we
talk about this and that for perhaps twenty minutes.
Alex, I learn, is almost my age, her sixteenth birthday
falling in late September. She tells me about her parents—her father is a writer I've never heard of but

whose adventure game books have made him a fortune, her mother is a teller at a bank—and I tell her a little about mine. After a while it starts to grow cold, and rubbing our hands, we move back indoors. The mob have finally deserted the kitchen, so Alex and I take charge here, sitting for a while on the counter beside the sink. When we're ready to leave, Alex dictates her telephone number, and though neither of us has a pen or any paper, I do my best to memorize it.

"Do you have any brothers or sisters?" she asks matter-of-factly, and I almost seize up for a minute.

"A brother," I tell her. "But you wouldn't care much for him. He's nothing like me at all."

6 TONY

Over breakfast next morning I'm doing my utmost to be nice to him. "How was detention?" I ask in all innocence.

"How was it?" Nick gazes up from his plate of eggs with a look of complete disbelief. "How do you think? Like a vacation." Scowling, he goes on eating.

"Detention?" Our mother, who has been dashing back and forth getting ready for work at the hairdressing salon she co-owns in Milton, suddenly stops dead, aghast. Detention is almost a taboo in our house, a word as vile as any obscenity. Far better to be caught drunk or smoking or stealing. "What happened?"

"It was nothing," Nick tells her. "Rees thought I was talking during homeroom when I wasn't, that's all. He mistook me for someone else." He is glaring at me as he says this.

Sometimes, I think, in his way, Nick is no better than a tenacious Staffordshire bull terrier clenching some filthy rag between its teeth. His foaming jaws lock together, he won't let go, there's really no reasoning with him. Seeing us exchange this dark look across the breakfast table, our mother sighs brokenly as she pulls on her coat. "You always used to do things together. Why can you only fight these days?"

"No one's fighting," I say brightly. "We just—"

"We have different interests now," Nick interjects. "You wouldn't want us to be identical all the time, would you?"

For one terrible moment I fear she's about to say yes. Then she lowers her head, checking her keys. "I'd just like you to be closer, that's all. There's nothing wrong with that, is there?"

"Of course not," I tell her.

"Definitely not," Nick mumbles through a mouthful. "But it's only natural we'll go our separate ways in the end." As he's speaking, it strikes me that he's wearing his hair exactly like mine, very slightly spiked up with gel, and I wonder what on earth his game is; he generally lets his hair lie flat. Seeing this takes me back years to the pins bearing our names and the labeled clothing. I never did tell our mother how Nick used to switch shirts and sweaters between our rooms. At the time she would have just laughed it off, and now she wouldn't even make sense of it.

From outside there are two sharp blasts of a car horn—our father waiting to drive her to work—and she says see you later and hurries from the kitchen like one of Pavlov's dogs to the bell. After we've heard the car head off, Nick and I sit in silence for a while. I don't want to be the one who hits out first, so I stir what's left in my teacup and say, "Maybe she's right. We used to be closer than we are now, didn't we?"

He nods, avoiding my eyes. "Only because she made us that way . . . because she made us do the same things."

"Yes, but we *are* alike in so many ways."

"Are we?"

"Sure we are. Sometimes I—" This is something I think about twice before confessing. "Sometimes when I look in the mirror, the way people do, I get the strangest feeling I'm someone else, not me at all."

"Really?" He sounds unimpressed. "That's never happened to me."

"And sometimes when I look at photographs of us— old ones—I have trouble making out who is who." I'm doing my best to be conversational here, but it's clear he still holds his detention against me, and I quickly give in. "So if we're so different"—I turn on him—"why are you wearing your hair like mine?"

"My hair? God help me, Tony. Can't I do with my hair anything I want? Didn't this used to be a free country or what?"

"Is something else eating you?" I'm suddenly faintly angry at him, ready for confrontation again. "Apart from your blaming me for what happened yesterday."

"Blaming you? That's not it. That's not what this is about. I'm just sick and tired of—" He stops there and leans back, holding himself in check, boiling inside but speaking calmly. "What's frustrating is the way everything falls into your lap," he says. "I have to work like a slave for everything, and everything comes to you on a silver platter."

"Not true," I tell him. Of course it isn't. How can he

believe such rubbish? Is he out of his *tree?* "Everyone
gets what they work for." I shrug. "Even *I* have to work
for it."

"Then why are your grades always so much better
than mine when you spend about half as much time
studying?"

"Because," I explain, "we have different aptitudes.
Different gifts. That's what *makes* us different. Why are
we having to even *think* about this? If you really want
the truth, if I spent four times longer in training than
you do, I'd still be four times slower on the track. Why
not just feel good about what you're good at and stop
sulking over what you're not?"

He looks at me for a long cold second, then rises from
the table in a flurry. "Where are my Nikes?" he says
flatly, distractedly. "Have you seen where I left them?"

• • •

At school, Vicky seems kind of standoffish and distant
toward me, only half there when I speak to her. I'm
wondering whether something I said yesterday has upset her. Then, as the bell sounds for first break and we
wander outdoors through the locker rooms together,
she says, "That brother of yours really had me going
this morning."

"How so?"

"Did you see how he's made himself look today?" She
makes a face: sheer exasperation. "Really I should've
known—I'm so used to seeing him jogging past my
house lately."

"What happened?" I ask, suddenly on yellow alert.

"What's going on with you two?" she says. "Are you out to get one another or what?"

"Just tell me what happened."

"It's only that he caught me off guard at the gate. Honest to God, it should've clicked it was Nick, not you; but I saw his hair and moved toward him, and before I knew it, he'd thrown his arms around me and kissed me. Quite passionately." She looks too unsettled to be amused. "I could tell by the way he kissed that it wasn't you."

"We are very different," I say faintly, my mind spinning. "In some ways more than others."

"Was that his idea of a joke?" she goes. "Well, *he* seemed to think it was funny. Believe me, Tony, whatever's going on between you, I don't want to be caught in the middle. Do you follow my drift?"

"Sure," I say, and stand there lost in thought for a time. Strangely, I don't feel shocked or even surprised by the news. Watching us from across the yard, his back to the field, is Nick. He stands with his hands in his pockets, smiling. I stare back at him and shake my head, though for the moment I can't think of what I could say to him that would make any difference. Then, from one of his pockets, he slowly draws a black plastic comb and with exaggerated sweeps of both hands removes the spikes from his hair, combing it flat.

■　■　■

"Now will you believe me?" I ask Vicky on the way home from school. The rose garden on Forest Hill causes me to sneeze yet again. "Do you still think I'm making things up about him?"

"I never said that," she replies. But she sounds as uncertain as she did yesterday when we almost lost our tempers with each other. This time, when we stand at her gate, she doesn't invite me inside for coffee.

"What are you doing for the weekend?" I ask, remembering the interschool sports meet.

"Didn't I tell you? I'm sorry. My dad wants to take us to the coast for two days. There's an apartment on the front in Scarborough that one of his friends rents out through the summer. Do you mind?"

"Would it change anything if I did?"

She looks at me, then down at her shoes. She is standing now on the other side of the gate, which is solidly closed between us. "Don't you think it'll be good for us, though? Not seeing each other for a change?"

"In what way will that be good?" I ask.

"It'll help clear the air, for one thing. You have to admit—well, we don't have to spend *all* our time together, do we? Shouldn't we appreciate each other even more when we *are* together if we go our separate ways now and then?" She sounds more hopeful than confident. In fact, when I think of it, she sounds like my brother.

"If that's what you want," I go.

"Are you angry at me?"

"Why should I be angry?"

She hunches her shoulders. "You sound as though you are."

"I'm fine," I lie. "Don't worry about it. Have a good time at the coast."

"Tony—"

But before she's managed to say anything more, I've turned away, trying not to show how agitated I really feel, and I'm heading toward St. Dominic's Grove, walking as fast as I can to work off a sudden rush of adrenaline. Even before I've reached the brow of the hill, I realize it isn't Vicky I'm annoyed with, but him. Although it makes no sense, I can't stop the thought that his kissing her this morning has soured things between Vicky and me, as if the joke was part of some bigger, more devious plan. When I reach our development, I notice, in one of the gardens, a Beware of the Dog sign, and chained to a kennel some distance beyond it a sleeping Staffordshire bull terrier. Although in the end I just ignore the dog, walking past at a clip, I still have to fight an urge to throw something at it, just to see what would happen.

■　■　■

At home I loll in my room for a while, bashing out a few angry chords on my guitar while an Iggy & the Stooges CD plays, a twenty-five-year-old recording that wipes the floor with the hollow nonsense everyone at school is still listening to. Even Nick thinks my tastes are eccentric, but what does he know? (He still has posters of U2 on his wall.) All he wants in life is to fit in with everyone else, as if that's all there is worth striving for. In fact, for all his talk of being his own person and doing his own thing, he'd rather be someone else—but never mind, I don't even want to *think* about him.

In the early evening, about five, five-thirty, everyone starts arriving from work. Dad, who works at Halifax

Property Services advising people about mortgages (but who also introduced me to the Stooges, which if nothing else proves there's life after day jobs), salutes me for some reason as I pass him on the stairs, heading down. I've decided by now to head over to Keith Dent's, since Keith's dad's garage contains a recently installed pool table that never seems to be out of service on weekends.

As I grab my jacket, a mock-leather blouson (not real leather, because Vicky has a thing about animal welfare) from its hook inside the front door, our mother asks if Nick's on detention again. I tell her yes, probably, even though I know he's really still training. Then she asks if I'm in such a rush I can't even stay for supper, so I have to shrug and say sorry, yes. In the fridge there's a potato knish and a can of 7-Up cold enough to numb my fingers, which I juggle into my pocket for later. Seizing the hot knish from the microwave, I kiss my mother's cheek, which seems to make up for my leaving as she arrives, and set off.

Outside it's still warm, but a cooling breeze cuts through the development, so I keep my jacket on as I go. On the threadbare patch of grass they call St. Dominic's Square, a handful of kids from the year below me are playing baseball with what looks like a slat from somebody's fence. The shops just beyond are already closed up, their windows and doors sealed with corrugated iron shutters to keep out the vandals.

It's such a pleasant evening, I decide to walk the whole distance to Keith Dent's (Keith lives on the other side of Milton in the Rosemount development) and not bother with the bus, even though it's just arriving as I reach the stop.

There's no sign of the car at Vicky's, and assuming they've already departed, I continue straight up the hill, straining a little before the brow, then down toward Milton Green. Perspiring now, I drag the 7-Up from my pocket. As I reach the first houses in the new development that surrounds the school, a voice somewhere away to my right calls out.

"Nick! Hey, Nick! Don't move! Stay right where you are!"

There's no one in sight, and it's hard to tell where the voice is located for the noise of the traffic rushing along the main road. Perhaps I haven't even heard correctly. Then I notice a house that faces the road from a junction mouth on the edge of the development: There's a girl at an upstairs window, waving, though all I can make out is the pale oval of her face. On impulse I glance back over my shoulder, thinking she means someone else, but there's only the traffic, and in any case the girl is calling at the top of her voice, "No, dolt! *You!* Who do you think?"

Everything happens at a clip after that. The girl disappears from the window, sharp as a light bulb going out, and by the time I've taken two swallows from the 7-Up can, she's appeared downstairs and is jogging along the pavement to meet me. Even before she comes up close, I've gathered I don't know her, but that she thinks she knows me. She's certainly what I'd call pretty, in a sort of very natural way, as if she doesn't need to think about it and doesn't spend four hours trying to hit the correct cosmetic note before showing her face in public. If she has on any makeup, it's not obvious. Her hair is as dark as her eyes, which are somewhere between green and brown, and she's wearing a striking white headband with a baggy white 501 shirt and faded, slightly raggy cut-off blue denim shorts. I notice, without staring, that both of her knees are grazed, and I'm trying to compose myself before explaining that she's made a harmless mistake when she kisses me on the lips and stands back, taking me in with a look that feels like a wave of warm air.

"How are you today?" she says.

"Oh, fine. . . ." For a moment I'm at a loss.

"Not moving too fast for you, am I?"

"Too fast? Noooo." I smile and fidget. But my name isn't Nick, I almost exclaim, at the last minute biting my tongue. "How're you today anyway, uh uh—"

"Alex."

"Just testing," I go, and she laughs.

Then there's an unnerving silence—we look at each other, and the light in her gaze seems to flare at me, though I'd swear she hardly knows it herself. At the same time I'm absently crushing the 7-Up can in my fist before I realize it's still half full, and the liquid is dribbling all over my fingers and wrist.

Alex can't help noticing this, but makes nothing of it. "Were you on your way over to see me?" she asks. "Then again, I never gave you the address, did I?" She puts a forefinger to my nose and presses. As she does so, I cross my eyes, making her grin. "Was that you trying to phone me this morning?"

"Probably," I say, undecided how I ought to be playing this.

"Thought so. But I never get out of bed for the

phone, certainly not at *that* ungodly hour. On vacation I never rise before ten. So I pulled the covers over my head until the damn thing stopped howling at me."

It's clear that she knows Nick, but for how long and how well? Is there something between them I should be aware of? Has Nick ever mentioned me to her? My mind clouds with a hundred warped questions. I'm beginning to feel slightly awkward just standing here, so I begin to walk slowly toward Milton town center, away from her house. Alex keeps pace with me.

"As a matter of fact," I tell her, "I was going to play pool at a friend's. Would you like to come along?"

"Pool? Why not? I've never played pool before. You could teach me."

"Easy as falling off a log," I tell her. Then I remember it's me—Tony Lloyd, not Nick—who usually turns up at Keith Dent's unannounced. Even if I could somehow fool Keith—and I don't believe for a moment I could—he's still seething at Nick for that phone call, the phone call *I* nearly got lynched for. If she turns up with my brother, there's no telling what might take place. "But pool's not such a great idea, really," I go. "Not on a lovely evening like this. The table's in some garage—dark and dingy and hot—and it won't be much fun. No, I think we could skip that. Unless you have other plans."

"Me? Nope. No other plans." She takes my arm, and all at once I realize there's no time to lose: Either I *become* my brother, at least for tonight, or else I come clean before I'm out of my depth.

Then she says, "Yeah, it was really fortuitous—is that the word? fortuitous—meeting you last night at the party. Suddenly I feel like my time here won't be such a drag after all." After a pause she shoots me an expectant look. "So where are you going to take me?"

"The movies," I say, almost without thinking. It strikes me, even as I speak, what a wise idea this is. Until I've managed to think everything through, what I need most is a chance to lie low where no one will notice or recognize me. "There's a new Julia Roberts at the Screen. I'm sure someone said it was well worth catching."

"Isn't it going to be hotter—and darker—in there than your friend's garage?" she wonders. "On a lovely evening like this, wouldn't you rather be doing something outdoors?"

I consider this for a minute. "The Screen has really great air-conditioning. It's practically outdoors as it is."

Alex shakes her head, perplexed. "Are you sure you're not busy? You're kind of distracted, Nick, aren't you?"

"Just surprised to bump into you," I say truthfully.

Some distance ahead there's a car waiting to exit a junction on our side of the road. The car, a battered gray Fiat, is familiar, and I almost stop dead in my tracks when I see it. At the wheel is Terry Mulligan's brother, Phil; in the passenger seat next to him, elbow jutting from the open window, is Terry himself. Both are members of Nick's circle. It's hard to tell which way they're about to turn, since neither of the car's indicator lights is on. After a moment Alex tugs at my sleeve.

"What's up, Nick? Everything all right?" Then, as the Fiat turns left toward us, she waves to catch Phil's eye.

"Hello there!" she goes, and to me, "Those are your friends from last night, aren't they?"

There's little doubt in my mind they'd have missed us if she hadn't kicked up such a fuss. But the Fiat is crawling along the curb now, slowing as it draws nearer. The game's up, I think, but at the same time I'm flattening down my hair as best I can, trying to look aloof, unconcerned.

"How's tricks, Nick?" Terry Mulligan says. His head and most of his upper torso are squeezing out of the window. "Good to see you two still hitting it off after last night." His brother Phil leers and chews gum but says nothing, instead revving the engine three or four times as if anxious to get going. "Don't do anything I wouldn't do, though. Don't get yourselves locked in any dark cellars. See you around, heartthrob!"

Both Terry and his brother are guffawing like donkeys as they speed away along the main road, burning oil that forms a noxious cloud above and behind the car. If what they're laughing at is some sort of joke, I can't see where I've missed it.

Watching them into the distance, Alex shakes her head disenchantedly. "Tell me truthfully, Nick, are they *really* your friends? I mean, honestly, you're so much better than them; you could *do* so much better."

Ironically, this is something I've told him myself many times, as if he gives half a damn. They're an unclean influence, is more or less the message I've delivered; hang around with smokers long enough and your own hair and clothing reeks too. Get out before it's too late.

"They're just acquaintances," I tell her. "Just something to do now and then."

She nods, unconvinced, and we walk on, though I still have no idea where we're going. As we near the town's shopping center, Alex pulls off her headband, roughs up her hair, and sings a verse from a current hit song, and I realize that each time I look at her, Vicky seems farther away. If I allow this to continue much longer, the truth is going to become harder to break.

So I clear my throat, meaning to come clean, thinking, Yes, the time is now, but the florist's on the main street is open later than usual tonight, its doors flung wide open to let the air in and the potpourri of scents out, and I'm struck by a sneezing fit, coughing and dragging for air. By the time Alex manages to drag me clear of the shop, my eyes are smarting and waterlogged. In the doorway outside the drugstore she pushes a clean handkerchief into my hand and says, "There. You poor thing. What was that all about? Hay fever?"

"I guess. Or an allergy. Sometimes the summer is murder."

She smiles sympathetically. "Funny it didn't hit you at the party last night when we went and stood outside in the garden. The scent there was just overwhelming."

"Well, it comes and goes." I shrug without much conviction.

"Still." She unfolds her arms in a long, luxurious stretch, which seemingly lasts forever. "It was wonderful out there, wasn't it? Just the two of us?"

Which is when I know there's no way on earth I can tell her I was never there at all.

7 $\overline{\underline{\text{NICK}}}$

There's almost exactly an hour to go before the first race—the 1500—when the nerves in my stomach begin tightening. Until then I'm on the verge of being anxious only because I'm not anxious: There's no pre-match tension, even though this day is all I've been able to *see* for three months through the haze of training.

Three hours before race time I wolf down the largest mound of spaghetti I can manage before taking a doze on a pool raft in the shade on the patio, and wake some time later wondering whether I shouldn't have prepared some other way. Apart from being bloated with carbo-hydrate—wouldn't it be better to fast before racing? Maybe I've got this all wrong—I'm lethargic and slow, rested when what I really need is an edge. Ideally what I'd like would be a long, quiet afternoon alone, perhaps thumbing books and magazines while the tension in my gut slowly takes hold. By the time I reach the bus stop, the stiffness still hasn't passed from my limbs, so I sit on a grassy bank nearby and massage my calves and thigh muscles and take several large deep breaths, which I hold down until the pain spreads through my chest and head.

There are three other schools involved today, all from the region. Downstairs on the bus, the only other passengers are a couple of blue-rinsed old biddies with passes, and I take the backseat for myself and try to think who I'm up against. There's a rumor that Billy Mayhew, who was at middle school with me before Milton Green, will be running in the 800 for Calderwood. If so, he's the one to watch, because not only does he kick off at speed, often leading from the front, but he's able to shift gears nearer home, accelerating like a sprinter with a mission. Then there's Carl Fenton from St. Mary's, the Catholic school near Milton Green. The word is he's likely to do something in both races, and because he edged me out by a nose in the 1500 last year, I know I'll have to stay on his case until the last.

Forest Hill comes and goes as I sit in the back, taking stock of my chances. A rose garden awash with vivid color near Vicky's catches my eye, though I've passed it every morning on my run without noticing. I take in these houses one by one, wondering whether Alex is anywhere near. Last evening I called the number she gave me two or three times without any reply.

Yesterday she was all I could think of. It was as if something about her made me want to run faster, to take Forest Hill in record time before running around the school yard three or four times for good measure. Then I saw Vicky Riley closing her gate as she set out for school, tossing her bag across her shoulder. The sun lined the crown of her head, bleaching her hair pure blond. God knows what made me do this on impulse, but suddenly just saying good morning didn't seem half enough; I wanted to throw flowers at her, sing her a song about what I was feeling for Alex, and although she caught sight of me at the very last minute, she'd already opened her arms as I threw mine around her, kissing her firmly on the lips.

The thing that hit me, when I let Vicky go, was her shocked, astonished expression. Her mouth sagged open, she wiped at her lips with the back of a hand but said nothing.

"Sorry," I told her brightly. "But isn't this a fantastic day? Just look! Hope everything's well with you too! Sorry, can't linger, I'm in training. . . ." And with that I was off.

It wasn't until later, when Tony gave me that look— you know, that *look*—of his across the school yard, first break, that I sort of realized how it must have seemed to them. Of course they didn't know about Alex; they couldn't know what I was celebrating.

Later, during lunch break, I was playing softball with Terry Mulligan and Gary Pitts when I saw them again. Gary was catching while I fired in these curve balls that would take off Terry's head (Terry was batting) if we were using a proper hard ball instead of this sorry sponge job. For once, instead of ducking or being hit, Terry connected with the ball, hooking it beyond the field and into the yard. It bounced three times before Tony trapped it with his foot, staring at it, then over at me, just glaring at me.

"Hey, Tony," I went. "Will you toss us the ball back?"

At which point he turned smartly away, leaving the ball, so that I (being pitcher and fielder) had to run and collect it. "That's all right with me," I yelled after him. "Running's what I'm good at, remember?"

You could tell from the way he walked away, not looking back, how badly insulted he felt. Of course he'd assume the worst about me. Doesn't he always? After all, I was the one who first noticed her, soon after we moved to St. Dominic's. During those first weeks I even invited her out once or twice, but my nerves were so shot by the time I'd summoned up the courage to even speak, she probably didn't know what I was talking about. Looking back, I think the worst mistake I made then was confiding in Tony. One night we sat in his room for an hour—this was the only time I remember really talking to him without fighting—while I explained what I felt and he advised, as an older brother is supposed to.

It was summer that first year here when I found out (not from Tony but from Vicky) that they'd been seeing each other for weeks. I never bothered having it out with him, because by then I already knew his game. In life, as in the dream, it is always the same. Tony always has to be first. Sometimes I even wonder if he went about wooing Vicky Riley just to spite me. Wooing is just one of the many things that brother of mine excels at.

Speak of the devil. Somewhere past the brow of the hill, I catch sight of him walking down toward Milton Green High. He's alone, which for him is unusual, but perhaps he's arranged to meet Vicky at the games. I'm inclined when I reach my stop to wait for him, but I'm not sure I want to break my concentration so near to the race. Instead, I jump from the bus, wave back up the hill, and turn from the main road into the housing development that half hides the school. It's probably my imagination, but the instant he sees me, Tony seems to freeze and withdraw, as if wishing for a hole to hide in. Then, standing his ground, watching me, he waves back sort of reluctantly.

Almost as soon as I see the private roads near the school jammed with vehicles, I know I haven't lost the edge after all. The pit of my stomach turns over, my skin prickles faintly. There are two chartered buses as well as many cars blocking the street outside the main gates, many of them double-parked, and in the near distance there's the sound of several hundred cheering, screeching voices.

Passing through the gates, I wander down the school yard until the athletic field comes into view through a gap between the science and art buildings. The crowd is almost as large as it sounds, though there aren't any seats and the spectators—nearly all of them kids from the four schools, waving scarves and banners in their own colors—are standing around the edge of the field nearest the yard or else along the wire fence where the road is.

At the moment there's a high-jump event going on. From such a distance I can't tell who's jumping, except that she's in Calderwood's all-white outfit and too stocky and short-legged for this event. As her heel strikes the bar, which wobbles, thinks twice, then drops, there's a ripple of oohs and aahs from the crowd and then sympathetic applause. I stand awhile longer, taking everything in until my stomach tightens again, and then I head indoors to the locker rooms.

There's an atmosphere in there you could cut with a knife. Competitors from all teams are either changing or else sitting in their outfits on the long, scratched, and faded wooden benches, their bags and coats on hooks above their heads, hardly anyone speaking except in occasional grunts. Billy Mayhew nods as I enter but says nothing, and I mumble hello in reply. He's wearing all white like the others from Calderwood: His team could be extras from *Chariots of Fire*. There's a haze of steam from the shower area too, which lends the changing room a feeling of dreamy slow motion. Someone has a cassette player on: Public Enemy.

Draping my own bag on one of the hooks, I change into Milton Green's colors (yellow tank top, black shorts) and my Nikes and flop down on the bench, studying my hands and knees. My hands, when I rub them together, feel colder than normal. No one makes eye contact with anyone. It's crazy when you face facts, but what we've heard from members of the staff in assembly just lately would make anyone believe someone's *life* depended on who wins and who loses, and now you can really feel the pressure at work. I shoot a look over at Carl Fenton, who doesn't even know I exist.

In the end it's Mayhew who breaks the deadlock. To me he says, "So. I hear you're down for the 800."

"You heard right," I tell him.

"Which means you're up against me."

"I guess."

"Good luck," he goes, then, smiling, "You'll need it."

"So will you." I smile back. "Up yours."

It's a relief when, ten minutes later, some official with a whistle slung around his neck turns up to call competitors for the first race, the 1500. Mayhew isn't in this and remains seated. There are two runners from each school, the other Milton Green representative being a junior, Michael Batts, who is slower than me. We file silently from the changing rooms and outside, where factions of the crowd boo and cheer while we make for the vacant center of the field to warm up. Minutes later we're summoned to take our positions on the track, and in the deafening silence before the gun goes off, I can feel the school—only mine; none of the others are here anymore—watching, willing me. The crowd is so far away now. You can almost hear a sniff, the flap of a flag, the faintest creak of bone or muscle as the seven other runners and I hold still in our lanes, suspend breath, listening for the starter's trigger finger.

Everything slowly turns blank; suddenly no one in the crowd has a face. All I can see are rooftops with jutting TV aerials in the streets beyond the school. "Right," I go through gritted teeth. Then the gun fires and we're moving like greyhounds from a trap.

From the start there's a blond-haired athlete I don't know in navy blue (St. Mary's) who takes the lead but doesn't know what to do with it. He's quickly displaced by Batts, whose running is all elbows and straining head twists that by rights should crick his neck, though at least he sets a pace that tests the field. About halfway around the first lap I'm lying fifth, and Batts is being challenged by a kid named Wing Lao from Abbotsbridge High who manages to keep up without killing himself. Then there's the noise of the crowd, harsh and roaring like the sea trapped inside shells pressed to both my ears, and their faces—slack-mouthed, wide-eyed—are smeared like paint as I pass them.

Ahead of me Wing is overtaking Batts on the bend where the track veers along by the fence near the road. Batts is still elbows and head shakes. Several spectators are gathering to watch outside the fence. Scarves are being tossed in the air. From the corner of my eye I see someone wave in the street—and then Fenton's moving forward from the rear, so I shift up a gear to keep up with him. By the time we're nearing the end of the first lap, I'm in fourth behind Fenton, Wing, and Batts, and I don't need to waste a backward glance to know the others are fading. Already, so soon, there are four of us in it and my nerves are no longer driving me: I'm in charge now, the wind in my face, my breath a hot and sharp knife in my throat.

Then Fenton steps into the lead, fending off the others as if they don't count, and I'm forced to accelerate again. Maybe he senses I'm the only real threat; he'll remember the scare I gave him last year, and his plan is to throw me earlier this time, not allow me a chance to cut in on the final straight. He knows from experience how I can finish, and wants to take it out of my legs early on.

And all at once you can *feel* him pulling forward and Batts and Wing slipping farther back behind us, and for a second or two I actually imagine I'm slowing down. This time as we near the half-lap stage, the crowd's roar is just another sound in my head, like my breath or the rush of my blood. Fenton is probably six or eight strides ahead, but not increasing the distance. I'm ready for him if he tries. I check behind me once, very briefly, and Batts and Wing are as far back again while the others are scattered even farther afield, the blond from St. Mary's at the rear.

The next thing I know, Fenton's checking me over *his* shoulder and accelerating once more, straining to open me up completely. The road sails past on my right in soft focus, the crowd's cheers are submerged, underwater. I push myself harder to keep him in sight, knowing that if he escapes now, it's over. My chest is on fire, my legs threaten to cramp. This is harder than anything I've faced during training, but suddenly I sense I can stay with him as long as I ignore the pain. Fenton is now at full tilt, perhaps ten or twelve paces clear, but I'm matching him stride for stride while the field stretches out behind us like slow, disconnected railway carriages.

After 800 meters he's visibly at his limit. His head is thrown back, his arms are pinwheeling. What's more, we both know he doesn't have a finish: If I can keep within range until the fourth and last lap, I'll be able to take him. Wing is maybe ten or twelve meters adrift now, while Batts has slipped farther out of it still to a clear but distant fourth.

As for me? I'm sailing, outracing the pain, trying to summon up that sensation again, the thrill of breaking the finish-line tape. At the half-lap stage, where the crowd is at its loudest, I'm already closing on Fenton. He's burned himself out too early, you can tell, and for twenty or thirty meters I gradually reel in his lead until we're shoulder to shoulder, so close his breath seems even louder than mine.

It isn't his breathing I hear, though, but the crowd. Even these few hundred scattered along the field's edge sound like thousands in my ears, and at the bend where the eight lanes begin to run parallel to the street, I cast a quick glance toward them, beaming, elated.

And it's then that I lose it, because that's when I see— quick as a flash frame in a film—Tony and Alex together in the street just outside the fence. I can't make out their features exactly, but at this stage in the race all my senses are heightened: my lungs overloaded with air, everything blurred and yet strangely, sharply in focus. What I see in that instant is enough to tell me everything: Tony watching the race intently, Alex leaning against him, watching Tony, her fingers playing lightly through his hair. It's only a momentary distraction, but the shock is so great, I might as well have stumbled over a rock.

The first thing to go is my rhythm. Somewhere between glancing at the road and back at Fenton I've lost my stride, and I stumble; my concentration snaps like elastic and then I'm threshing my arms for balance, toppling forward.

The moment I hit the ground on my hands and knees, I'm aware of the thunder of stampeding cattle—the sound of the others overtaking me one by one. I'm down for no more than five or six seconds, just long enough to draw a succession of deep breaths and propel myself upward again, but already I'm trailing too far behind to recover what I've lost. Already Fenton has quadrupled his lead.

Just as I set off again—there are still three runners behind me—I cast a glance backward toward the fence. In the street outside Tony and Alex are gazing deep into each other's eyes; they don't even seem aware of what they've done. Then I notice others, faces from Milton Green, shaking their fists and shouting angrily after me, "Come *on*, come *onnn*, get back *in* there. . . ."

Suddenly they hate me for losing. Just for a second it's written clearly in their eyes. Through the haze and the soundtrack of rushing ocean breezes, I can see and hear everything perfectly now. It isn't me they care about at all, it's winning, being first, no matter what the cost or who to. The fact that I was so close doesn't figure. Trying is nothing if nothing comes out of it, that's what they're thinking.

"When the time comes," Tony's voice rings out somewhere deep in my mind as the dream comes flooding back and I picture him standing over me again, fists clenched, teeth bared, "when the time comes . . . *I'm going first.*"

With some effort I'm able to fight my way back into fourth, just behind Batts, for the fall has taken it out of me and cramp has crippled my legs. As I'm rounding the bend onto the home straight I see Fenton raise his arms and punch the sky, victorious, and make a barrel of his chest as he breaks the tape. It makes no sound, and for a moment everything stops. The roar I hear then is the crowd in my own imagination, applauding me, *my* victory.

By the time I cross the line, I'm practically at a standstill. The official in the pale-gray track suit pats my back and says, "Bad luck, son, never mind, maybe next time," while I sag with my hands on my hips and gasp in pain for air. Everything is spinning. At last the cramp forces me to sit on the ground, and I know I'm out of the 800 too. There's a lot of activity around me, most of it centered on Fenton. Kids from the crowd have hurried across to offer congratulations; even members of staff hum around him like wasps at a honey pot. Everyone loves a winner, I think, and when I next look over toward the roadside, there's no sign of either Tony or Alex.

8 TONY

B elieve me, when he finally overstretches himself and tumbles and hits the ground, my heart goes out to him. Until then he's put up such a gutsy fight, it gives me a feeling of brotherly pride just to watch, really it does. For a time I stand awed, forgetting our differences. Then they hit the bend on our side of the track and everything seems to fall apart: He twists around to check who's behind him, tries to push himself harder—but, to be fair, he's never got what it takes to catch the leader, even though he's closed the gap slightly before tripping over his own feet. Anyone can see the leader has enough in reserve to coast home without effort.

"Damn it," I go under my breath.

Alex strokes my hair, seeing nothing but me. She just isn't interested in sports. Which is just as well, because I'm sort of uncomfortable watching Nick run and tumble right there in front of her. As the race is won and

Nick limps home, I turn away, gathering her hand in mine. Last night we saw the new Julia Roberts at the Screen after all, and talked incessantly afterward while I walked her back to her cousin's house.

"Have you seen enough?" Alex asks. "I thought you wanted to watch the games."

"I've seen what I came for," I tell her. "Let's go to Ferdinand's."

Which is a legendary Italian coffee and cake shop in the town center where the espresso is always good and the ice cream second to none. All along the glass counter there's an astonishing array of desserts: chocolate-covered cannoli, moretto, truffles . . . and gaudily handwritten signs listing the ice-cream flavors: marron glacé chestnut, nocciola, cappuccino . . . There are Italian tricolor flags on the walls and tapes of Pavarotti piped at low volume through speakers half concealed in far-flung corners by rubber plants. Alex orders a hot-fudge sundae while I sit with my elbows on the table watching her. Widening her eyes, licking her lips, she sinks the long, slender spoon into the depths of her glass. She smiles toothily at me before her first mouthful, and Vicky is so far away, it's impossible to imagine what will happen when she gets back.

Alex says, "Tell me about this brother of yours. Are you close to each other?"

"Well, so-so." I wrinkle my nose, wave a hand. "Depends on what you mean by close."

"Whether you talk to each other . . . do things together." She takes another spoonful of fudge sundae and makes a face that says: heaven on earth. "Your brother's older than you, isn't he?"

"No." I'm quite adamant here. "I'm the eldest."

"Really? I thought you said he was older. At the party I thought you said—"

"One of us must be mistaken then." This sounds so abrupt, I lean back in my seat, smiling to lessen the impact.

"Me, I suppose," she says. "But you're not a lot older?"

"There isn't much between us. We're in the same year at school."

"Close as that?" She nods as if this solves or explains something. "It's only that sometimes there's rivalry between brothers—or brothers and sisters, whatever—who're born so close together. My two older sisters were twins, in fact. Both have moved out and are married now, and are very good friends, but when they were small, there was constant competition between them." She pauses. "It never became vicious or nasty or anything . . . but there was always this sort of struggle for attention."

"Whose attention?"

"Oh, anyone's. Mom's, Dad's, even mine." Briefly she is lost in the memory, then her eyes refocus and she's back in the now. "It's as if they both needed *all* the love and didn't want to share it. Was there ever any needle between you?"

"Uhm, well. I suppose . . ."

"You'll have outgrown it all now though, I'll bet. What did you say his name was?"

"I didn't. But it's Tony." Which, to say the least, feels slightly awkward on my tongue. Her questions are beginning to make me feel restless, hunted. "Where's this leading?" I ask. "This business about my brother."

"Nowhere in particular. I'm interested in him, that's all."

"Why so?"

"Because you told me I wouldn't like him. It made me curious."

"When did I say that?" I ask matter-of-factly.

"At the party the other night. You remember." She's frowning at me over her hot-fudge sundae glass now. She is fascinated, confused. "Really, Nick, sometimes you're so . . ."

"Yes?"

"I don't know." She shakes her head slowly. "Can't put my finger on it. You have such an odd—such a selective memory. Some things just go right out of your head, don't they? Creative people are a little like that, I suppose; my dad used to be hopeless if you caught him in the middle of writing something. He'd drag himself around all day long with this kind of other world in his mind; he couldn't see the real world at all—everything seemed to just wash over him. He was so impractical."

"Well, I'm not creative," I tell her. "My grades are fine, but I haven't any burning desire to write books or paint pictures."

"But you act as though something's preoccupying you. Are you sure you're okay, Nick?" Her spoon, piled high with ice cream, pauses midway between the glass and her mouth, and a dollop drops on the red-checked tablecloth. "Maybe it's too early to say so, but if there's something you need to get off your chest . . ."

After this she goes back to her dessert, and the clink of her spoon in the glass sets my teeth on edge. Staring at the tablecloth, I imagine a game of chess: My king is cornered by both white and black queens, which for some reason have taken the same side against me. But chess was never my thing, and the only game I ever won was the one I played against myself on a pocket set during a train ride to London. Finally I look at Alex again, at her warm, expectant face, and I shrug.

"No, I'm fine," I go. "Nothing's bothering me."

You can tell right away that she's less than convinced, but she skips it and instead begins outlining her father's adventure-game plots to me. I listen intently, lulled by her voice. Many of these plots are of the dungeons-and-dragons kind and involve lost and found treasures, magic rings, anagrams and arithmetical clues, and acts of unrivaled bravery. Her father has written more than twenty of these. One in particular that grabs me concerns a feud between two brothers that lasts many years and leads to ultimate catastrophe: Both possess supernatural powers that enable them to burn anything, bend and distort and explode anything, bring anyone they wish under their influence, create monstrous beings out of nothing—powers that in the end they turn against each other, threatening western civilization in their selfishness.

"That's quite a feud," I marvel. "What was the cause of it?"

"Jealousy." Finishing her dessert and pushing the

glass from her, Alex adds laughingly that the story was inspired by her sisters. "To say how innocent *their* differences really were, it always amazes me how Dad rethought it all, turned it into something else altogether. But I suppose there's rivalry and rivalry, isn't there? With some people it's harmless enough, but with others . . ."

"Yes. I can imagine."

"But I suppose it depends on who they are and what made them that way in the first place," she says, and I nod.

9 <u>NICK</u>

I'm on my way home before the competitors are out for the 800 meters, and it isn't a pleasant journey, believe me. Each lurch of the bus sends a knifing sensation through both my legs, which are still riddled with cramps, and I can't even get a seat downstairs, which is full of shoppers heading home, so I'm forced upstairs— and the climb up brings on the cramps again.

Even after I've massaged the tightness from my calf and thigh muscles, I feel I've been kicked in the chest by a mule. God knows what I *look* like. All I know is that I felt fine, within reach of everything I'd slogged so hard for, until I saw those two together. When you're winning, I guess, it's easier to ignore the pain.

At least the ride home gives me time to think, though it's too soon to be clear about anything. Did Alex seem so happy because it was *me* she thought she was with? Or has Tony charmed her away, telling her everything? Either way, *he* knows the score, and there's no way I can forgive him in my heart. Some nerve he had, bringing her to the games just to flaunt her. What he's done once again is what he always does, pushing me out of the way to make room for himself.

Almost as bad is the way Billy Mayhew was gloating when I collapsed in the locker rooms afterward. If I'd had the strength, I might've swung for the airhead. While I'm sagging on the bench, my head down and hair drenched with sweat and my breath short and ragged, he goes, "Really, Lloyd, if *that's* how you feel after warming up, just wait till we get to the race!"

I look at him but say nothing; can't think of anything *to* say. But if looks could kill, his ashes would be scattered far and wide across the great athletic track in the sky by now.

"Only joking," he goes, and I nod, but for all that you can tell he means every word. Two minutes later, as soon as I've recovered my breath, I silently pack up my gear and walk out.

At home, stomping up to my room, I throw the plastic bag containing my things so hard against the wall, the vibration dislodges a shelfload of paperback books, a couple of which fracture their spines as they fall. Then I flop on my bed, my head on my hands, and stare at the ceiling, gritting my teeth. All my clothes are sticking to me. There's a pounding in my head, behind the eyes, that makes me feel I'm still running at full tilt. It takes me perhaps half an hour, sprawled out like this, to calm down. At least our folks are not home, a relief since I'm in no mood for explaining. I'm still trying to decide what to do, if anything, when the telephone rings downstairs in the hall.

It's probably for *him*, is my very first thought, and I choose not to answer. But supposing, just supposing— and I imagine a scenario where Tony comes clean about everything and Alex decides to phone me to apologize, to confess to me what a dreadful thing she's only just discovered he has done. It's *me* she wants, not him, provided I can really forgive her, and now that she understands what Tony's about, she feels betrayed and used and wants never to see him again. On the phone I'm very cool and composed and I tell her I'll think about what she's saying. Please call soon, she begs, and through a yawn I tell her I'll think on it.

The phone must be on its eighth or tenth ring by the time I finally peel myself off the bed and head down. Even before I reach it—still in no hurry—I'm halfway back to reality and I *know* that Alex won't call me now, not even if she knows the whole story. Tony has this way with girls, always has had—and if he's won her over, she won't see anything from my side too readily. For another three or four rings I stand watching the phone, wondering. Then I answer.

It's Vicky. There's a very faint click on the line before she speaks, which tells me she's not calling from a local phone. "Is that Nick?" she asks.

"Yes it is. Hello, Vicky. Where are you?"

"Didn't he tell you? *Honestly.* We're in Scarborough. We'll be back probably late tomorrow night."

"How's everything there?"

"Okay," she says. "The weather's great. *Très* hot. But the streets are very busy. Given a choice I would've stayed to watch you run, though. How did it go?"

"Not so well. I came in fourth."

"That doesn't sound so bad. Fourth wasn't last, was it?"

"Not quite. But I could've done so much better. If only . . ." I trail off, almost biting my tongue. In my mind there's a very clear image of Alex running her fingers through Tony's hair. "Things just didn't work out the way I'd planned, that's all."

"Ohhh. What a shame." She sounds genuinely sorry. "Better luck next time, though, eh?" Then the brightness returns to her voice. "Ah well, I'd better have a word with you-know-who since I'm on the line. Is he there?"

"I don't think," I begin, and then seize up, as if the breath has been jolted from my body. I take a deep breath to calm myself. "Hold on, I'll just see if he's around. Won't be a minute."

Laying the receiver down next to the phone, I walk steadily through to the living room. This is a large, light-filled room with white walls and teak bookshelves and a framed print of a famous painting by Turner on a wall facing the window. The painting is of a ship adrift at sea in a storm; you almost can't see it, in fact, for the crashing waves and bucketing rain.

On another wall, above the fireplace, is an oval, gilt-edged mirror that no one in the family likes, but that our mother has kept because it belonged to her grandmother. For a few seconds I stand in front of it, lost in my own unblinking stare. There's a blemish to one side of my nose that could soon become a pimple, and my skin has a drawn, almost pasty look about it, as if all the training has worn me down instead of building me up. There isn't even a hint of tan. Reflected in the mirror behind me is the open living-room door, and out in the hall the telephone table. Roughing up my hair with both hands, I say aloud—loud enough for Vicky to hear my voice, but not necessarily every word, "Tony? Vicky's on the phone for you. Really? Hold on, I'll be right there." I'm lost in the mirror as I speak.

Then I walk leisurely from the living room, flop down on the seat and pick up the phone. My heart is racing, but everything else is under control. It's something like that prematch tension all over again, a tension that eventually you can learn to make work *for* you instead of against you.

"Vicky?" I go. "Sorry about keeping you waiting. I was in the middle of doing something."

"Lounging, I'll bet. Falling asleep in the sun, doing nothing, which is about all you're good for."

"That's it. You've got me."

"I know you, that's why." She pauses. There's a change in her voice, which sounds slightly small, slightly hesitant on the line. "Is everything all right?" she asks.

"Of course. Why shouldn't it be?"

"You know well enough. We didn't exactly sign off on the best of terms. I thought you were angry with me, the way you stormed off."

"Me? Angry? No way." I haven't the faintest idea what she means, but I'm taking my chances. "It was nothing. How's Scarborough?"

She tells me what she's already told me. *Très* hot, *très* overcrowded. But this time she adds playfully, "You should see my tan."

"You're tanned already?"

"By the time I'm finished here I will be. Then you should see it."

"Don't," I go, forcing a laugh that sounds like Tony's, a sudden breathless wheeze of air from a bellows, "don't even make me *think* of it. It's bad enough I couldn't come with you."

"Never mind, it's only for the weekend."

"But weekends can seem a long time, sometimes. A lot can happen in a weekend."

She sighs, "Did you see Nick run? When I spoke to him just now, he didn't sound too happy about his race."

"He did well," I go, and suddenly I'm aware of how much power there is in my hands—power to say anything about anything I want as long as she believes I'm him. The absolute truth about Tony and Alex, the race, the real reason for my failure. My head is swimming with possibilities. In my limbs there's the same adrenaline rush I had the moment I edged Fenton on the last lap. But instead I just shrug and say, "The luck wasn't with him. I was so disappointed, and he did really brilliantly well, but it wasn't his day."

"Sounds very generous, coming from you," Vicky says.

"How so?"

"Oh, *you* know. The way you usually run him down. The things you say, the things you accuse him of. But we've been over this before, you don't need me to . . ." She pauses, letting the moment pass; but something in my chest has just tightened sharply. "It's just nice to know that you can feel for him when he's competing, that's all. It proves there's still something between you."

"What do you *expect*?"

"Peace, perfect peace, is what. I wish you'd both just grow up and shake hands and have done with it." You can tell she is angry at Tony over something, though she's doing her damnedest to sound carefree. "Really, he isn't nearly as dark as you paint him, you know."

"Is that why you called? To put me in my place?" There's a spoiled note that comes into his voice when he's on the defensive, and I've caught it exactly. "Isn't it the wrong time to be going over this? Shouldn't you— shouldn't we both be enjoying our weekend?"

"Look, let's forget it," she goes after a moment. "It's only that we didn't have much time to talk before I left. I'd rather be there with you any day. Now that we've cleared the air, I feel *so* much better. We're always clearing the air lately, aren't we? How about you?"

"Me? I'm fine. Just fine." Then as an afterthought, "I guess his kiss won you over, am I right?"

She laughs. "Who're you? The green-eyed monster himself? I'll have you know the kiss was perfectly innocent."

"That isn't how you took it at the time." Her stunned,

openmouthed look is still very clear in my mind. She couldn't have been more astonished if I'd slapped her. "In fact, you didn't know *what* to make of it."

"Ah, but after a while it's easier to see things more clearly. At first I was a little confused, that's all. Really, Tony, there's no need for jealousy. Sometimes I think you misread what he does; you only see the downside of everything. Loosen up."

"Sure," I say solemnly, secretly thrilled to know what she's thinking, that she doesn't see everything through Tony's eyes. "I'll try. No hard feelings. Have a good weekend, what's left of it."

"Sure I will. And you too."

By the time we've hung up, I'm certain she hasn't a clue she's been speaking to me. The thought makes me feel—not guilty exactly, but slightly unclean, as if I've been spying, reading through someone's private diary or letter. But in another way I'm elated, on top of the world. It isn't even as though I've gained anything by spying, but at least I'm less angry, and more in control again, and my failure at the interschool sports meet doesn't hurt so much.

After the phone call I'm thirsty and dry, so before heading outside for the last of the sun on the patio, I root through the fridge for a 7-Up I bought a few days ago. It's no longer there—someone else must have claimed it—so I take one of Dad's Heinekens instead.

Out on the patio I drag an easy chair from the spreading shade into sunlight and collapse into it. Perhaps because of the sun's warmth, or the drink, or the exhaustion I'm feeling, it doesn't take long before I'm drifting toward sleep. For some reason I dream of a scene in a film I once saw: the chariot race from *Ben Hur*. This time, though, the scene is different from my memory of it, because Tony is driving one of the chariots and I'm at the helm of another. There's dust and heat and the pounding of horses' hoofs, and there's a wild look in Tony's eye as he grits his teeth and whips his horses. At this point we're going neck and neck. His chariot is the one with blades on the wheels, which gradually slice the spokes of my own wheels to sawdust, and as the chariot starts to collapse underneath me, I wake up in a sweat.

10 <u>TONY</u>

Just before five we're caught in a light shower as Alex drags me across the pedestrian mall in Milton. Half-way between The Body Shop and War on Want (she says she buys most of her clothing at thrift shops) the rain begins, and by the time we're huddled indoors, drying ourselves in a cool blast of air-conditioning that will probably lead to pneumonia, my hair is properly flattened, like Nick's. I don't bother trying to rearrange it.

Having checked and rejected the trousers and jackets in War on Want, Alex takes my hand and leads me back where we came from, toward HMV next door to The Body Shop. HMV, although occupying two large floors, is crowded as a nightclub and twice as loud. The CDs, mainly hip-hop and rap, are cranked up so loud I can only mouth to Alex, "Let's go somewhere else. I know a better place for records than this."

By which I mean somewhere quieter, a place where browsing doesn't require earmuffs and a bullet-proof

vest. Honest John's is known in these parts for its secondhand vinyl LPs and unhurried, jazzy atmosphere,
and on weekends people meet here before moving on
to the movies or pub or wherever. It's in a side street
around the corner from the new, squeaky-clean mall,
an old red brickwork building with flaking red paint on
its windows and door and a fusty smell inside. The rain
has stopped by the time we're heading down there, and
the streets sparkle blindingly in the sun. Even from a
distance you can hear sounds through the open doorway that no other record shop in town will ever play:
Lou Reed singing "Venus in Furs" from the first Velvets
LP. As soon as we step indoors, though, I'm tempted to
about-face and walk straight out again, because the first
person I see is Gary Pitts, one of Nick's circle. He turns
to see Alex and me near the entrance. A broad, rather
dumb smile lights up his face.

"Tony," he goes. "How's everything?"

Alex looks at me, puzzled. I clear my throat and say,
"You made a mistake, Gary. This is Nick you're talking
to."

"You're kidding," he goes. Then, running both hands
back through his bristly hair, "That's amazing, really it
is. Sometimes it's just impossible to tell the difference,
you're both so—"

At which point I interrupt him, before he can go any
further, in the only way I know how, by feigning a
coughing fit. For perhaps a full minute I'm doubled
over, hacking into my fist, going blue in the face. Alex
pats my back, convinced that I'm choking. When I finally come up for air, she pushes a strand of hair back

from my brows, fixing me with a sort of concerned expression.

"You poor thing. *Now* what? Another allergy?"

I sniff and try to regain my breath. "Must be. It's probably the dust in this place."

Gary shakes his head, still marveling at his error. The ploy seems to have worked. He broadens his smile for Alex. "Hello there again. Didn't I see you at the party the other night?"

"Yes," she admits. "It was . . . *interesting*. That was where Nick and I met."

Gary nods. To me he goes, "So what are you doing later on?" He indicates a bulletin board on the wall above the Indies section where handwritten and photocopied flyers announce coming local events. Among them is one for a local—the only—rock venue, The Abyss. A band called The Mad Egyptians is playing there tonight, he explains: all guitars and drums and distortion, a wall of sound like the old days before the synth wimps took over, not a midi in sight. "What do you think?" he asks us.

"Sounds like heaven to me." Alex grins, game for anything.

"Me too," I say. I've seen the band once before and my ears are still whistling faintly. We arrange to meet at the club at nine-thirty, and when Gary takes his leave, I give a sigh of relief I can't disguise.

"Something up?" Alex asks. When I shake my head, she frowns, watching me closely. "Is he another of your friends?"

"You could call him that."

"Then tell me, Nick. Why is it that every time you set eyes on one of these so-called friends of yours, you turn white as a sheet? You reacted the same way when we saw those oddballs in the car yesterday."

"White as a sheet? Me? You must be imagining. Gary's just something to—"

"Something to do now and then?"

"Yeah, that's about it."

"That's what you said yesterday." She shakes her head, skims through a few secondhand LP sleeves without really seeing them. The Velvet Underground song has now finished and something by Kraftwerk begins. After a moment Alex turns to me again, this time with vague, troubled eyes. "Nick, is there something you're not telling me?"

"Like what? About what?"

"About—you and your brother, for instance."

There's really no getting away from it, but it's becoming harder to be truthful the further this goes. So I throw up my arms defensively. "Didn't we just spend half an hour discussing my brother in the coffee shop? Haven't we been all through this? What more can I tell you?"

"Why Gary thought you were Tony, for instance." And as she speaks, you can see the understanding rise in her eyes like a lifting fog, and she nods to herself, as if seeing clearly for the first time. "Are you really so much alike that even your friends can mistake you?"

"We have our similarities. This kind of thing happens all the time."

"Would *I* be able to tell you apart, do you think?"

Slowly, I inhale and exhale. "There's no comparison,"

I tell her. "All right, so there *are* similarities—physical ones at least, I'll admit that. But we're brothers after all; we're in the same year at school. What Gary meant was, anyone can make a mistake, especially when you think how I must've looked to him just now, all messed up by the rain when he didn't really expect to see me—and bearing in mind how dark this place is. . . ." I wave at the shop's dim interior to prove my point. "Really, Alex, I don't understand what you want. What are you *accusing* me of?"

"I'm not," she says meekly. "I'm not accusing you of anything."

"But you're making me *feel* accused."

"All I'm doing is asking, Nick. Why are you—why are you angry with me? I'm curious only because I'm interested in you, because I want to know more about you, that's all." She seems genuinely troubled by my outburst.

"Let's forget it," I say after an interval. The Kraftwerk song sounds stuck in the groove. "Just take it from me. Tony and me, we've nothing in common. One of these days, who knows, you'll meet him and then you'll see for yourself." Though hardly superstitious, I'm tempted to cross my fingers at this point. "I'm sorry for overreacting. It's just that while we're together, he isn't the first and only thing on my mind. There are other things to talk about, really there are."

With a smile I take her hand and give it a firm squeeze, and she nods and the moment passes. All the same, I can't help feeling the lie has gone too far and there's no way of stopping it now. I'm on a sort of runaway car ride where the brakes have gone, and because we're heading downhill at top speed, there's no way even throwing it into reverse will help.

"Here," I say, guiding Alex toward the racked sleeves of oldies. "Did you ever hear anything by The Stooges?"

■   ■   ■

Past the center of town, heading from Milton toward Wakefield, the squeaky-clean pedestrian thoroughfares vanish and the streets become inexplicably darker. There's a worn-down, vandalized look about some of the houses out here; many of those with For Sale signs outside also have broken or boarded-up windows. There are still a few shops and amenities though: a library few people use anymore that seems to be closed more than open; several fast-food takeouts; a pub called The George with a reputation for Friday- and Saturday-night brawls.

On James Street, The Abyss is set in a basement beneath a pool hall. As soon as you reach the top of the bare stone steps leading down, you know the place is aptly named. At the bottom is a small booth where a russet-haired punk girl stamps your wrist with the place's name and date when you pay to enter. Alex seems a little nervous at first when we head inside, unless she's just fazed by the time-warped atmosphere: Some of the posters on the bare brick walls date from the early 1980s, some of the music from earlier still.

The club is really just a spit-and-sawdust bar where Mohawks and skinheads share tables, nodding their heads over their beers while an earsplitting sound system belts out Wire, The Clash, David Bowie. Everyone—but everyone—is smoking; you can feel your pores clog the minute you walk in. Half the place is cordoned off for a dance floor, at one end of which is a knee-high stage where the band is just setting up and soundchecking. Occasional blasts of acoustic feedback interrupt the songs in the bar. The bartender, a tall, pale rake with sucked-in cheeks and an Aladdin Sane haircut, looks at me twice when I order the drinks— Bacardi and Coke for Alex; a Heineken for myself—but he never asks for ID. Three quarters of the kids in the place are still juniors or below.

"Is this where you bring all your women?" asks Alex, straining above the noise to make herself heard.

I ruffle her hair and guide her toward a corner table with two empty seats. "Only the ones I want to impress."

"Is that so? In that case, where do you take the others?"

"You wouldn't even want to *hear* about that," I go, and she laughs. "There are nightclubs in town where New Men who *really* want to impress girls can go, but my reasoning is, if you can stand me here, you can stand me anywhere."

"Oh, I suppose I could stand you anywhere, Nick." She leans nearer to give my hand a quick squeeze.

We sit for a while listening to the crash of old songs, the occasional howl of feedback from the stage. Though it's pleasant enough to be here, tapping my knee in time to the sounds, making eyes across the table at Alex, I can't help wondering how I'm going to break the news about this to Vicky; or when the time comes, how I'm going to explain Vicky and Nick to Alex.

But those bridges I'll cross when I come to them, I think. This is now and that's then. And four or five minutes before the band starts playing, I lean across and kiss Alex on the lips, quite spontaneously. Then I lean way back in my chair and look at her. She doesn't look surprised in the least, and if she is, she's not showing it. All she does is chew her bottom lip and look at me fondly for a long moment. Then she says, "Damn good thing I got myself locked in that cellar."

I don't understand the significance of that, but rather than ask I hold my tongue, in case it's private, something between her and Nick.

"Me too," I tell her, and then look away across the bar. Many of the punks are now shoving back their chairs, seizing their beers, and making a beeline for the stage, where The Mad Egyptians are just kicking off their set. There are no preliminaries, no announcements: The band just plug in their guitars, crank everything up, and let rip. Their noise is a sort of barely controlled chaos, as if the drummer were keeping time to a machine gun or jackhammer. As I raise my glass to my lips, I can feel it vibrating against my teeth.

Alex is already on her feet and signaling me to follow her toward the stage. I'm on my feet and halfway across the bar when someone thumps me firmly in the back, then drapes an arm about my shoulders.

It's Gary Pitts again, this time with a slightly glazed expression and a beery smell on his breath. Cupping his hands over my ear, he bellows at me, so loudly his voice feels like a sharp metallic probe inside my head, "It's on!"

"What's on?" I go. "What are you talking about, Gary?"

"The party." He frowns. "Same place as before. Didn't Terry call you about it?" From his pocket he pulls out a door key and waves it at me and grins drunkenly, knowingly. "Property of Bob Clark, bless his heart. Soon as the gig's over, Phil and Terry are picking me up outside. If you and your lady friend want to come . . ."

"Sure. We'd love to. Where did you say it was happening?"

"Same place as before. Where you met her."

"All right. See you there." During a lull between two Mad Egyptians numbers, I tell Alex, "There's a party right after this if you're interested. Same place as before."

"Where? At the house?"

"That's it. At the house." Now we're getting somewhere. "Where we met."

"Why not?" She shrugs. "If it turns out like the last one, we can always stand out in the rose garden again, can't we?"

"Sure." I nod, picturing myself doubled over, sneezing and coughing, then trying to explain myself afterward. "Sounds absolutely fine by me."

"This town," Alex says with a shake of the head and a cynical glint in her eye. "Life here's just one long endless party, isn't it?"

"That's how it's beginning to seem," I agree.

Then the noise begins again.

11 <u>NICK</u>

Something in the dream of the chariot race is still stuck to me, even as I stand twenty minutes in the shower, trying to wash both it and the feeling of disorientation away. But it has nothing to do with the race's outcome: There's nothing to remember once my chariot disintegrates under me. All I can think of is Tony's face, his narrowed eyes filled with loathing, his lips drawn back from clenched teeth. This, let me tell you, is exactly how he appears in the dream I sometimes have about the endless night before we were born. In all these years, when you get right down to it, he's changed so little, and he still wants only one thing: to be first.

By the time I'm drying myself, I feel clearer about everything—clearer about what I should do. Dressed only in boxer shorts, I wander across the landing to Tony's room and open his closet, pausing to picture what he was wearing today at the games. For a second or two I close my eyes and see: Alex turning her fingers through his hair, and Tony . . . in a collarless black leather blouson (I have one almost exactly the same) and a jade polo T-shirt or sweatshirt with faded blue Pepe jeans. Though I never noticed what he had on his feet—who would?—my guess is white sneakers or black oxfords with Argyle socks. After a brief search, I find the oxfords tucked under a night table next to his bed.

Fortunately there's a second jade shirt like the one he was wearing on a hanger in his closet. Apart from that, everything I need I can find in my own room. My denims are older than his and worn through at the knees, but they'll do. After dressing in these and the T-shirt, I gel up my hair to look more like his, then head downstairs to phone Gary.

While I'm perched at the phone table, dialing, I stare at my knees through the holes in my jeans and remember again how Alex looked that night climbing out of the cellar, dusting herself, making light of it. There's a lump in my throat now almost all the time when I think of her, partly because she was so easy to meet and is suddenly so hard to find again; and partly because this has happened before, more times than I want to remember. Alex isn't the first girl he's stolen from under my nose; nor was Vicky.

"What do you want?" says a voice on the telephone line. I'm connected to Gary Pitts's house, and I recognize the voice as his kid sister Monica's. Not yet fourteen, Monica is fearsome. The last time I set eyes on her, she was in the school yard beating the living daylights out of some Hell's Angel boyfriend she'd just discovered was two-timing her. "Who is it and what do you want?" she goes. She doesn't even keep up the pretense of politeness. "If it's Gary you're after, you're better off trying one of his weirdo friends. He's not here."

"I *am*," I tell her, "one of his weirdo friends. Did he say what he was doing today?"

"Wait a minute. He wrote something down in case anyone called. It's somewhere around here." There's a delay of some moments while she looks. The rustling of paper sounds like electrical interference on the line. Then Monica says, "He's written something about a party in the Rosemount development. That's over near Milton somewhere. There's an address and directions, but his handwriting's so godawful . . ."

"The party was two days ago," I explain. "Are you sure that's the message?"

"This has today's date written on it."

"Are you sure?"

"Of course I'm sure. I'm looking right at it, aren't I? Do you think I'm an idiot or something?"

"Is there anything else?"

"Wait a minute. Good God, his writing's so scruffy I can't . . . wait a minute . . ." I hang on while she murmurs some part of the note to herself over and over again. All the while she's grunting and groaning to make sure I know this is putting her out. Finally she says, "*Really*, someone should teach that lummox how to write. *He* might be able to decipher this mess, but I can't."

"Never mind," I go. "You've already been *such* a great help. Not only that, but you've brightened my day no end."

"Are you kidding?" There's a pause, then she says, "Why don't you take a flying one at the moon?" and hangs up.

For the next few minutes I sit in the shade on the patio with my coffee, trying to fix in my mind what to do. Even if Gary had answered, I wouldn't have been sure what to ask, or how, and now that I'm made up like Tony, I have only the vaguest idea why. It could be nerves or anger or both that cause the coffee cup to tremble in my hand as I raise it to my lips. Some of the coffee spills on my knee, but it isn't hot enough to scald. Then the phone rings indoors and I race to answer it, hoping that it's Alex, knowing it won't be, deflated when I realize it's only Terry Mulligan.

"Tony?" he goes. "Ah, Nick? Not interrupting anything, am I?"

"Like what?"

"*You* know. It's just that Gary said he'd seen the two of you in town this afternoon. Are you having a good day?"

"Sensational."

"Won't keep you then. Better let you get back to her. Tell me, is she really as good as she looks? Har har." His docile laughter is almost the final straw; in my fist the receiver feels fragile, easily crushable. After a second or two Terry settles himself. "Just calling, in case you didn't know about the party tonight or you can't make the Mad Egyptians gig. We'll be picking Gary up from The Abyss at eleven. If you're coming later, it's the same house as before, the one Bob Clark's dad refurbished."

"I'll be there," I say. Then, as an afterthought, "One way or another, *we'll* be there."

"That's the spirit. I knew we could rely on you. Bad luck about the race today, by the way."

"Never mind. These things happen."

"Yeah, perhaps they do. Though I heard Billy Mayhew wasn't so impressive in the 800 meters. What they say is, he came first without winning; he did it without any real competition. He was slow and out of condition. Real shame you couldn't have been there, Nick. From all accounts, you would've buried him today."

"So it goes." I shrug. "Win some, lose some." But the news, though I'm trying to sound come-what-may, makes me feel ten times worse. If only I hadn't fallen when I did, if I hadn't been *made* to, I might well have wiped the smirk from Mayhew's mouth once and for all, and now the chance has slipped away for another year.

■   ■   ■

It's that time of night, now, when the dingy streets near The Abyss crowd with drunken groups leaving pubs for tacky nightclubs and parties like the one in Rosemount. Friday and Saturday nights are the worst times to be stranded here waiting for a bus, and in fact many services are curtailed after ten o'clock because of vandalism. As I reach The Abyss, there's a scuffle on the street outside the ground-floor pool hall above it, though it doesn't last long and the two tattooed, fortyish men soon move on, trying to settle their differences in blunt, slurry voices.

I find a patch of shadow in a doorway across the street and ease into it, where I won't be seen from the club. In a way I'm sort of lost here, not really sure what I'm doing or why; but at the same time I'm convinced Alex is about to appear, arm in arm with my brother. Something tells me it isn't enough for Tony to step into my shoes, stealing her away from me; he wants more than that, the risk turns him on—otherwise why would he bring her to watch me at the games?

Far across town the church clock is striking eleven. Outside The Abyss the band is loading their gear into a yellow Vauxhall. Another car, a Fiat, pulls up behind it, and when I realize it's Phil and Terry Mulligan, I'm tempted to cross over and jump in—except that that's the very moment I catch sight of the others coming out, Gary Pitts, who looks booze bleary even from this distance, and behind him Tony and Alex.

Holding my breath, I step farther back in the darkened doorway until I'm leaning flush against the cold brickwork. There's no way on earth they can see me, which is probably just as well: God knows what watching them together is doing to my face.

Tony has his arms around Alex, who is laughing freely as if she's been drinking. She runs both her hands through his hair, then kisses him firmly but quickly on the mouth. Leaning from the Fiat's passenger side window, Terry Mulligan mutters something I'm unable to catch; then he and his brother Phil crack up simultaneously: Har har har. My hands, pushed deep in my pockets, form fists as hard as rocks. After several moments of fidgeting, Tony asking questions, Gary wobbling uncertainly on his feet, the threesome scramble inside the Fiat. At the same time I become aware of something leaning lightly against my right ankle: an empty milk bottle, which sort of spins away from me when I try to readjust my footing, and which I can't make a grab for lest they spot me. The bottle rolls forth from the doorway, down two stone steps, and smashes below me in the gutter. Phil Mulligan looks up from behind the wheel of the Fiat, but no one else pays any attention. Several streets away a dog barks at the noise, which sets off a chorus of other dogs, near and far. Finally they drive away, and my last impression is of Tony and Alex snuggling together in the back, his arm around her shoulders, the two of them trapped for an instant in the yellow Vauxhall's headlights as they pass.

■ ■ ■

It's little more than a ten-minute run to the house in Rosemount. By the time I arrive, the Mulligans' gray Fiat is already parked outside and the music is pulsing away like a headache. Sooner or later the properties down here are going to be sold and occupied, and the parties will move elsewhere to empty warehouses, boarded-up shops, or under the arches of unused railway bridges. For the moment, though, this seems to be the place to be seen at, judging by the numbers of cars in the street, easily twice as many as before.

The large front window flickers as I move toward it, the heads and shoulders of the dancers inside seeming to jerk like puppets, trapped in the strobe lights. It's dark in the street, but there's still a chance someone will see me loitering, so I turn from the drive down the side of the house. A couple of kids in the year below me stand leaning back against the wall here, smoking.

You can tell I've interrupted their conversation, though it's hard to imagine it being anything important, and I sense their eyes following me as I walk past. The tips of their cigarettes glow like beacons in the blackness. I can't see their faces—it's too dark—but I really don't want to. The younger they are, the more they seem to feel they have to prove. As soon as they figure I'm out of earshot, rounding the house to the backyard, their muttered conversation picks up again.

Next thing, I'm standing somewhere in the rose garden, which tonight seems even darker and more heavily scented than when I stepped out with Alex. There's a three-quarter moon overhead somewhere, but it's mostly obscured by thick cloud, and the only light is that cast from the kitchen window. Although the party is twice as busy this time, there's no sign of anyone in the kitchen, not even Phil and his automobile-appreciation society. All I can hear of the sounds indoors is a regular thump-thump-thump, no melody at all.

For a moment I wonder whether the thing to do next is take time to compose myself properly, then march indoors and confront them; let Alex see us together, let her know what he's doing and exactly how he's been manipulating her. But suddenly my nerves are jumping. I'm standing alone in the yard, dressed up to look like Tony, and although I'm still angry at him, I'm also cold and confused, not at all certain what I'm trying to prove. As a sort of nervous reflex, I flatten down my hair with both hands, the way it should be. Seconds later I'm scurrying for cover as, without warning, someone moves quickly through the kitchen and outside.

At the last minute, just before they step out into darkness and the door swings shut behind them, the kitchen light bathes their faces. It's him and her. Not that I'm surprised to see them; but I've been taken unawares, they've appeared before I'm ready. Falling to my knees, unable even to see where I'm landing, I find myself caught in what feels like a mass of overgrown rosebushes, surrounded by thorns, grabbing handfuls of spikes as I reach out to steady myself.

"It's darker than before," Alex says to him. Her voice is softened by drink, thick and slurry. "Isn't it wonderful though?"

"Mmmm," Tony goes. "It's mmmm . . ." And at once I realize he's fending off a sneeze; either that—his allergy is flaring up—or he can't decide how to play this, how to pretend he's reliving a scene he's never been through before in his life. "Mmmm, it's really, uh, *dark*," he goes.

Even as I'm swallowing down a cry of discomfort, I'm trying to keep from bursting with anger. Alex has known me—known him, known *us*—for barely two days, and already she's revisiting old haunts as if we first came here years and years ago. Spare me. My mouth is bone dry, my teeth clenched. If she dares to say Do-you-remember-when-we-came-here-before, I swear to God I'll explode in their faces.

There's a long, easy silence during which I count to ten while my hands form fists, almost without my knowing. The thorns claw at me, scraping my face and knuckles. Kneeling here, skulking, trying not to call out in anger and pain, I'm suddenly aware how calm and quiet

the street is, the party excepted, how deserted and far
removed from everything. St. Dominic's Grove could be
galaxies away. There isn't a star in sight. It's the end of
civilization, I'm thinking; it could be a desert island. A
breeze stirs through the yard in the dark.

Then Tony says, "You could easily forget where you
are out here, couldn't you?" It's as if he's stolen the
thought from my mind, as if he hasn't already stolen
enough. "All those miles and miles of fields."

"Yeah," says Alex. "It's like being at sea. Or lying flat
on your back, watching clouds pass over. Everything
floating."

"You've been drinking too much."

She laughs very gently. "You certainly know how to
charm a girl."

"I know all the right lines," he tells her.

"The truth is, tonight I'm intoxicated, but not the
slightest bit drunk."

"There's a difference?"

"In this case I'd say so." This is spoken with a sort of
meaningful heaviness, after which the two of them stand
backlit by the fluorescent glow from the kitchen window,
gazing deeply into each other's eyes, hands touching
faces. At this point I'm on the verge of snapping, threshing my way from the rosebed and marching across to
confront them, when Alex says, "Wait here, Nick. I just
need the bathroom. If I'm not back in five minutes,
you'll know which door I'll be locked behind."

I can tell by his silence, there's no way he understands
what she means by this. They kiss briefly, and then Alex
bounces indoors, leaving him alone in the garden. Once

she's gone, his shoulders drop slightly as he releases the tension he's feeling. He sneezes, then stands for a moment, fidgeting, flattening his hair with both hands. It's clear he isn't comfortable with this scene, so why on earth does he bother?

"What's the game?" I ask quite spontaneously, in a cool clear voice that makes Tony spring back in alarm. The light from the kitchen forms a halo about his head. "Is it really worth all the fuss when you know damn well I can spoil everything between you any damn time I choose?" I help myself up and start toward him, though the rose thorns try to claw me back, scraping the sleeves of my jacket, piercing my knees through the holes in my jeans. But the impression this simple movement makes on Tony is something to behold: He totters backward, one hand slapped across his O of a mouth, the other clutching his heart. When I draw closer, he blinks disbelievingly. Just for a second I mimic the way his hands are, placing one on my chest and one on my mouth. It's like gazing into a mirror, apart from the state of my jeans and the scratches I can feel on my face. I smile at him broadly, though I don't take much pleasure in any of this as I'm not in the best frame of mind.

"What the hell are you *playing* at?" he goes at last.

"What the hell are *you* playing at?" I reply like an echo.

"You scared the living daylights out of me. Don't ever do that again." In his eyes there's a look like the one in the dream as he seizes my jacket and drags me toward him. "Don't *ever* do that again, do you hear?"

"Don't ever give me cause to," I reply. "You knew what you were getting into, Tony. Why are you doing this to me? You knew I met her first, you *must* have known. Did you have to chase after her just to spite me?"

After a beat or two he lets me go. "I'm not," he says. "I mean, not spiting you. And I didn't . . . really didn't chase after her. The fact is, Alex came to me. She thought I was you, she made a mistake. And I thought—God knows what I thought. It's all so confusing. But I like her and she likes me and no one planned for that. It was an accident, Nick."

"A friggin' catastrophe. Something good happened to me, just once, and you really couldn't stand it, could you? You had to deny me even that."

Tony looks at me, shakes his head slowly.

"We'd better talk," I tell him. "But we can't really here. She'll be back in a minute. I heard her say so."

"You heard everything just now?" He doesn't seem surprised so much as angry, volatile. "Is that what you've been up to—watching us, listening? How long have you been following us then, spying? All night? Did you learn anything?" Half raising a hand as if to strike me, he quickly thinks better of it, and lets it falls slackly to his side. You can tell he doesn't know how to act, which way to turn, how to unravel the mess he's made. "What are we going to do?" he wonders.

"Let's talk." Taking his elbow, I steer him toward the house and indoors to the kitchen. "I know a place where we can settle this once and for all," I go. "I know the very place."

12 TONY

The first thing I'm aware of once Alex has dodged indoors is his voice, like a snake's, like a hiss filled with poison: "Why keep up the pretense? I'm going to spoil it for you anyway, I'm going to pay you back good and proper."

I've scarcely had time to absorb this when he lurches forward—at first I only hear, can't see him—and rushes toward me with such murderous intent I dodge backward, convinced he's carrying some weapon or other. As soon as he comes close and the light from the kitchen picks him out, I'm able to see exactly how murderous, how close to the edge he really is. His appearance is shocking, not only because this is Nick, but because he's so changed, so transformed. His fists are bunched, his face is a rash of scratches and smears. There's something of the mad dog about him that reminds me of his expression in a dream I occasionally have; a dream of the two of us before we were born. And I think: Is this really my brother?

After we've stood there awhile, nothing happening between us, I notice that he's wearing my other jade polo shirt and that the rest of his clothing echoes everything I'm wearing today.

"What are you *playing* at?" I ask him at last.

"What are *you* playing at?" he mimics.

I take a few seconds to collect my senses. "You scared the living daylights out of me, Nick. Don't do that again. Don't you *ever* do that again, you hear me?"

"Then don't ever give me cause to," he says, sort of menacingly. "Tell me one thing: Why are you doing this to me, Tony? You knew I met her first, you *must* have known the score before you got involved. Did you have to chase her just to spite me?"

"I didn't mean to spite you," I tell him sincerely. "If you must know, it was Alex who came after me. She thought—well, she mistook me for you, and I thought, well, God knows what I was thinking about, but it all got out of hand so quickly—"

"Don't give me that." His voice, harsh and flat, cracks down like a cat-o'-nine-tails. "You couldn't stand the idea of something good happening for me, could you, someone choosing me, not even this once. You had to deny me even that."

A deadly silence spins out, and as we stand there facing each other in the dark, it occurs to me we're much like two dogs playing tug of war with some highly prized rag; we're talking about Alex in her absence as if she were something with no voice of her own, no opinions. And if the tug of war continues, I think with a shudder, she'll be torn to pieces between us.

"How long have you been following us tonight? Did you learn anything while you were spying?" I ask.

He doesn't reply.

At long last I sigh and throw up my hands. "So what are we going to do?"

Nick seizes my elbow, roughly. Perhaps he wants to provoke me, make me react, give himself some excuse for a fight. "We're going to talk this through, but not here—she'll be back any minute." Already he's jostling me toward the back door, then inside to the kitchen, where the light makes me squint after the blackness outside, and he slams the door after us. "We're going to settle this once and for all."

"What's there to discuss?" I ask him. "I *know* I've stepped out of line, and I'm going to explain things, really I am. Do you think it doesn't bother me, keeping this going?"

"There's a lot to discuss," Nick says gravely. "We can talk in there, where we won't be seen together."

He's guiding me now toward a door across the kitchen, dark and old and heavy-looking with splintered oak wood and rusted hinges, which doesn't exactly complement the kitchen's modern décor. When Nick has unlocked and opened it, I see nothing inside but darkness. Then he flicks a switch just inside, and a light comes on and there's suddenly a flight of stone steps leading down to a grubby concrete cellar floor.

"We'll be okay down there," he tells me.

"Why?"

"Are you kidding? If you'd prefer, we can just wait around until Alex comes back, and then she'll find out about us the hard way. Fine by me, if that's what you want."

A little reluctantly, I follow him down, pulling the door closed behind me as I go. Even before reaching the bottom, I'm aware how the noise of the party has faded completely. The walls and floors of this place must be inches thick, so thick it's almost like entering a tomb. At the bottom there's the penetrating smell of damp and a litter of rubbish all across the floor: crates of old newspapers, cans of paint, empty wine bottles and beer cans. Everything seems to cast its own long, unnatural shadow, the cobwebbed electric bulb overhead is so poor.

To our right there's a sort of alcove, which suggests there's more to this place than meets the eye. Thinking of catacombs, I follow Nick toward it, but the alcove holds no secrets, only another door, this one with faded, stenciled lettering across it—you can just make out the word STORAGE—and two sturdy bolts top and bottom. The bolts are open, and Nick pushes the door gently and peers inside, though there's little to see except darkness.

"Some place," I say, shivering, rubbing my fingers. "Maybe they should have brought the party down here. Liven things up, wouldn't you say?"

Nick just looks at me, his face quite unreadable.

"What on earth made you choose this place to talk in?" I ask.

"Well, I thought it seemed—appropriate." He studies the scratches on his hands. "This is where we met, me and Alex. Didn't she mention it to you?"

"In a fashion. She sort of joked about the cellar, but I didn't really catch her drift. She seemed to assume I knew what she meant."

"She would, wouldn't she? As far as she's concerned, you're the one who let her out when she found herself locked in. You *are* me, in her eyes. There isn't anyone else."

"I—I suppose that's how it is."

Nick is perfectly silent for a minute; in the darkened alcove his eyes appear briefly like hollowed-out sockets; the sound of his breathing coats the cellar walls. Not for the first time in my life, I'm nervous to be alone with him.

"You never wanted to be me before," he says. "Why would you want to be now?"

"I don't," I tell him. "All I've done is improvise—make things up as I went along. This situation's all new to me. What would *you* have done?"

"I wouldn't have made myself out to be you."

"Wouldn't you though? Look at you, Nick, just look at yourself! You're wearing my *shirt*, for Chrissakes! And that jacket and jeans . . . Coincidence? Sure. Maybe *you* have some explaining to do."

But Nick shakes his head, clucks his tongue. "You've flattened your hair down to look like mine."

"You've gelled yours up to look like *mine*." Tit for tat. I clear my throat before going on. "In any case, it was raining. It couldn't be helped. But you can't expect me to believe *that*—" I ruffle his hair, which is hard and spiny to the touch—"was an accident."

"Accidents will happen," he answers mysteriously.

There's a look in his eyes I don't really recognize and don't trust. "All kinds of things happen that can't be helped."

"Exactly. That's exactly what I've been trying to tell you about Alex. No one knew she was going to happen; I certainly didn't."

"But you could have—you could've played fair."

I let out a sigh in exasperation. "Look, Nick, this is going nowhere except around in circles. Is there anything more to say, or is this all you wanted? Because if so, there's no point in my staying." I'm already turning away from the alcove when he makes a grab for my arm, digging his fingers in at the elbow.

"What about Vicky?" he wants to know. "What are you going to tell her?"

"The truth. What else?"

"And Alex? You'll tell *her* the truth too?"

"Sure. Of course. Do you think I'm happy about what I've got myself into? As soon as the time's right—"

"You want it all," he goes, and again I'm reminded of a dog, snarling between its moist, locked teeth. "You always wanted everything for yourself, at my expense. Even when we were kids you pushed me aside, held me back. I remember one year we were on vacation at the coast, an afternoon when our mom and dad took us to the beach. . . . A long cliff-top walk. But the walk led us through woodland, weaving up and down and in and out, and you couldn't see the sea until the very last minute."

"I remember," I say very faintly, wincing as his fingers firm their grip on my arm. "Yes, I think I remember. In

Cornwall somewhere. We were five or six then, maybe seven."

But he doesn't see or hear me as he continues. He is far away and hears and sees nothing but that day. "We were some distance in front of our folks," he goes. "Fifty yards or more, and our mother kept shouting, *Hold on, be careful,* while we walked faster and farther ahead. We were following a path that was covered with stone chips, and now and then there were signposts, so we knew we weren't getting lost. Then farther along both of our parents started shouting, *Slow down, wait there.* But we paid no attention, just kept hurrying on—and what we were doing was . . . Do you remember why we were hurrying, Tony?"

I nod, almost solemnly. "We were racing to see who would get there first. To see who would see the sea first."

"And who won?"

"Let go of my arm, Nick, you're hurting."

"Who *won*, I'm asking. Who got there first?"

"*I* did," I answer, and drop my gaze.

"Then how? I've always been faster; you've said so yourself. I'll tell you how. Because as soon as we were far enough in front to be out of sight of our folks, you knocked me down and ran ahead. And because of the way you pushed me, I went off the path and into a shallow ditch and down on my ankle, and after that there was really no catching you."

He seems to be waiting for me to respond, but what's there to say? I shrug and raise my hands plaintively. "So?"

"I never told them what happened," he says. "Even

when they found me struggling to get on my feet again, I said nothing about it. When they asked about my ankle, I told them I'd tripped. I've kept the truth to myself all this time."

"But why, Nick, why? What happened that day meant nothing; we weren't *old* enough for it to mean anything. Everyone grows up doing things they regret later on or being on the receiving end of things, but that's part of growing up. What do you want, an apology for what happened when we were six years old?"

"What I want," he says slowly, and you can tell he's choosing his words very carefully, "is for you not to take over. It's about time you made space for me. Gave back what you've stolen from me."

I'm flabbergasted by this. My mouth sort of wavers open, though no sound comes out, because I haven't the faintest notion what to say. Is this how he sees things? Does he really believe this is what I've been doing, that the way things turn out is always designed and the odds are stacked against him only because I've arranged it that way? It's as if his whole life he's been watching the world through dark glasses, as if he can't see anything for itself anymore. Worse, though, is the look on his face as he speaks, the blank, set expression: a look that tells me he's reached some sort of turning point.

The next thing I know, both his hands are on my arm and he's swinging me around and past his right side with such suddenness, I stumble and fall the instant he lets go. The force of his throw is enough to send me skidding across the dusty floor on my backside. This is all crazy, so unexpected that at first I don't even register which direction he's sent me in. I'm not even angry; I'm much too disoriented for that. But perhaps he's expecting me to come back at him, fists flying, because no sooner have I scrambled to my knees than he jumps backward, away from me.

Then I realize why. In an instant that feels like a guillotine blade whipping down, I see, and understand, everything. I've landed somewhere inside the storage room in the alcove—he's actually sent me careering several feet through the entrance—and Nick is jumping backward to give himself clearance from the door. "Nick," I go, but my voice is weak and breathless. And already he's pushing the door shut, the darkness blotting out everything, my view of the cellar beyond him, the world.

The door closes with a solid, permanent thud that vibrates through the walls, and as I fumble toward it, slamming the woodwork with both palmed hands, there's the sound of the two bolts crashing shut, one then the other.

"Nick!" I cry out, this time straining at the top of my lungs—but there's no answer at all except for the echo of my voice. I don't hear the party upstairs, and I certainly don't hear Nick leaving the cellar, if he does so. Just in case he's still on the other side of the door and can hear me, I count to ten, then knock twice and say, "Okay, Nick. Joke's over. You can let me out now. No hard feelings. Let's just say this never happened."

But when he doesn't reply and the door doesn't open, not in two or five or ten minutes' time, I know what I sensed from the first is true, that it was never a joke to begin with.

13 NICK

"Joke's over," he says. Joke's over. As if that's what he
believes this is about, why we're here. What's happened between us is only half serious, to be taken lightly,
laughed off. "No hard feelings," he says, as if *he's* in a
position to forgive and forget. Which means I've overstepped the mark, and if I'm careful, if I play my cards
right, he'll forgive me. "Let's just say this never happened," he says, his voice still threatening. At this point
I turn away, covering my ears with both hands before
his cries for help start.

By the time I reach the top of the cellar steps, I'm so
dizzy my head seems to be floating. Checking the coast
is clear, I lock the big old door and pocket the key, and
just as I'm finishing, the door between the kitchen and
the hall opens, the noise of retro-dance music swells,
and Alex sweeps in. She's taken three or four steps into
the kitchen before she sees me. Then her face seems to
slacken, her mouth opens speechlessly as the state of

my clothing and hands and face and exposed knees registers with her.

"Nick, what the hell have you done to yourself?"

"It was like this," I reply, talking a moment to inspect my hands. There are scratches like lifelines all over the place and both of my palms are bleeding. "It's so damn dark out there I couldn't see what I was wandering into. Just my luck to land in the roses, ha ha."

She rolls her eyes heavenward, takes a step nearer. "Honestly. Can't I leave you alone for two minutes?" She touches my face and frowns, as if seeing something there she doesn't quite expect. "Can't take you anywhere, can I? What *have* I got myself mixed up with?"

"More than you know."

"No kidding." She forces a smile. "But I'm glad."

"You are?"

"What do you think?"

There's a moment then while we gaze at each other, breath suspended, and I wonder if what she sees in my eyes resembles anything she might have seen in Tony's. After a moment she frowns and touches my brow, studying me so closely, I can feel myself flush.

"Are you—?" she begins, then breaks off. She's confused, on her guard.

"Go on. Am I what?"

"Oh, it's nothing. You're right. I've been drinking, is all." After a beat she nudges my chin with her knuckles. "It's just that for a second I thought . . ." She shrugs, laughs it off, whatever it is. "Anyway, you could do with a shave. A shave and a bath. Just *look* at you. Perhaps we'd better leave early. We're both a bit past it, and there's always tomorrow, isn't there? Things will seem different tomorrow."

"Sure," I say, in all honesty with some relief, because as long as we're standing here in the kitchen, there's always an outside chance Tony's cries will penetrate the thick cellar walls to seek us out. That, at least, is what I'm afraid of.

■ ■ ■

We stroll back through Milton mostly in silence, holding hands, my left in her right: Mine feels hot and slippery with sweat, or perhaps it's hers. After a while it's hard to tell whose is whose.

"Penny for your thoughts," she says as we pass the florist's near the end of the main street.

"I doubt they're worth so much," I tell her. But in truth I'm thinking that now that I have what I wanted—Alex back again—I'm unable to appreciate the fact, because all I can see in my mind's eye is Tony cooped up in the dark, and all I can smell and taste is the clammy, damp air in that cellar.

It's late, and the traffic through town is relatively light. You hear individual vehicles approaching from a long way off, and when they draw nearer, you can antici-pate the blast of cool air as they pass. Most of the houses in the Milton Green development are in darkness. My watch tells me it's ten before one, and I wonder whether our folks will be waiting up, worrying.

I'm quickening my step across a junction on the left when Alex stops sharply, tugging me back. "Hold on, have you forgotten where I'm staying?" It takes me several seconds to come to my senses. Of course I never knew, but I slap my brow with the heel of a hand as if I've just realized my error. "Sorry," I go. "I was miles away."

"That fall must've really shaken you," she says.

"Fall?"

"In the roses."

"Oh, that. Oh, yes." Though I know she couldn't have meant the 1500 meters, it's the only fall I can immediately bring to mind, the only one that counts. "God knows what I was playing at."

"You're all right now though?"

"Oh, definitely. Really no problem at all."

"Because you're so distracted. In fact, you haven't seemed yourself at all since it happened." We're standing beneath a streetlight outside her cousin's house, and the light is full in her face. She's watching me like a hawk, as though she's just sobered up with a jolt, or remembered some detail of vital importance, and it's easy to imagine her mind working overtime, a thousand cogs turning behind those dark eyes.

"Don't worry," I reassure her. "I'll be myself again tomorrow. Wait and see."

A long moment passes. Then she relents, leans nearer, eases her arms around me, over my shoulders, drawing me close. "All right," she says. "See you tomorrow then. But for the record, I really had a great time tonight. Did you? Of course you did. Thanks for everything, Nick." And she presses her lips firmly against mine.

I'm a little slow to respond, I'm so unprepared, but

after a second or two I manage to snake both my arms around her waist and return her kiss, closing my eyes because hers are closed. The tip of her tongue flicks against mine and I have no worries. But even as I slowly lose myself in the moment, Alex is pulling away from me, shaking her head, and my spirits are sinking rapidly, almost as if I know what she's going to say before she says it.

"No," she whispers. "Not like that. Kiss me *properly*, like you did before."

■　■　■

Next morning at breakfast I'm more distracted than ever since I hardly slept a wink in the night. Stirring my tea, I watch the surface bubbles crowd and collect and separate and re-form for minutes at a time. My whole body aches from the 1500; my skull feels paper thin, as if any sudden harsh noise will tear it apart. Across the table my mother and father are staring at me.

"It'll get cold," my mother says. "Aren't you interested in breakfast this morning?"

"Heavy night?" asks my dad, too cheerily. "To me this looks a bit like the morning after the night before."

"That's about the size of it," I go, not meeting his gaze.

"You must've been late," says my mother. "We didn't hear you come in, did we, Frank?—and the Clint Eastwood film didn't finish until twelve. Was it a nightclub? You know you're not old enough to go drinking in nightclubs."

"A party," I grunt.

"Even worse. Anything can happen at parties."

"Indeed," says my father. "Your mother and I met at one. Better watch your step, Nick, before something like that happens to *you*."

She punches him lightly on the arm, and even though it's obvious things are healthy and good between them at the moment—they go through phases—I'm unable to join in, to laugh at their horseplay, because I know that Tony isn't fast asleep upstairs in his room as they think, that his bed is still made, the sheets perfectly tucked, that he never came home last night. There's a slice of toast on my side plate that I can't face and can't even find the strength to butter.

"What about Tony?" my father asks, as if he can sense what I'm thinking. "Did he come home with you?"

"No. I—I left him behind at the party."

"The dirty stay-out. I expect he's still in a coma then. He didn't even groan when I called him for breakfast."

"Better just let him sleep it off," says my mother. "It's Sunday, after all. But he should have waited; only one more week of school to drag yourselves through and then you've got the whole summer to celebrate. Isn't that something?"

"Yeah, it's something." Stirring my tea once more, I watch the bubbles skirt to the rim of the mug. "Tomorrow I'll probably get detention again for that bloody disaster on the athletic field."

"But you couldn't help what happened; how could they hold it against you?" My father looks genuinely astonished. "What kind of minds would sneer at you for losing? Isn't competing the thing that counts?"

"Not if the school's reputation's at stake. You should have seen the way they were yelling at me after I fell. The staff as well as the students. They could've *killed* me for letting them down."

"But you didn't give up," my mother protests. "You got up and back in there, didn't you? You had enough about you to keep going, even after everything went wrong, and even *then* you came fourth, not last. What more could they ask?"

"A place among the winners." Just saying it aloud makes me wearier, because if you can't gain a place in the one thing you're supposed to excel at, what chance have you got? "Anyway, Tony won't let you down. He's top of the heap this year in practically everything but sports."

"Won't let us down?" my father exclaims with a note of irritation. "Won't let us down? Is that what you think *you're* doing?"

"Do you think that's how we think of you both?" my mother gasps. "That we'd ever set one of you above the other? To us"—she glances at my father for moral support—"to us you're both exactly the same."

"Can we talk about this another time?" I ask, nursing my head. Though my body needs to sleep, I know that my mind won't keep still long enough, because each time my eyes close, I'll only be able to see the same image: the change that comes over Tony's face the instant he sees I mean business, as I seize his arm and hurl him aside through the storage room door. For a fraction of a second everything's crystal clear, and you can see the understanding in his eyes: He knows he's gone too far, that he's pushed me once too often.

I'm still fuming at him for what he's done, even if I've reacted harshly. Some might say I've overreacted. But I meant every word of what I said to him last night: He *has* been trying to take over, no doubt about that. Perhaps he's so accustomed to having his way that he just doesn't see this and never did.

What happened that time at the coast, though, when he pushed me down and ran hell-for-leather to reach the sea first was only the beginning. Yet there was something else about that day; something I remember distinctly and didn't understand fully at the time, which explains why our parents were yelling for us to slow down and were almost in a panic by the time they found me sprawled in the ditch nursing my ankle.

Toward the end of the coastal walk the path became treacherous, flaking and cracked where the salt sea air had gradually eroded it over the years. Our first glimpse of the ocean came as the path escaped the trees and veered sharply downhill to the cliff's edge and the sheer drop beyond, a drop of at least eighty feet. There were DANGER notices posted everywhere, on both sides of the path before it petered out and at the slatted wooden fence near the edge, which vandals had torn down so that any unsupervised child could easily wander too far and go over. Because he'd been running, Tony might easily have overshot the break in the barrier—and maybe because they knew this route, our parents were still yelling, *Slow down, slow down*, even as they emerged from the trees with me in tow.

Tony stood at the path's end, thirty yards ahead, on the safe side of the shattered fence, signaling us to join him, shouting, "Come look, come look!" All I could really feel was anger. I never saw the danger, even though I knew that one-hundred-foot falls to the rocks were bad news. I was six years old and my brother had purposely hurt me to get what he wanted. My ankle throbbed and he'd beaten me to the prize, to first place. That was the only thing that concerned me.

Now, over breakfast, another thought strikes me about that afternoon, a thought I could never have appreciated then: If Tony hadn't pushed me aside, if I hadn't twisted my ankle— But I don't want to think it, I really don't, and squashing the thought like an insect, I stir my tea vigorously, take a large swallow, and rise from the table, excusing myself.

"What are you going to do with your day?" my mother calls after me as I saunter from the kitchen.

"This and that. Maybe run a few miles, work off some of this stiffness, visit a few people." This is terrible. Even I can't believe how humdrum it all sounds, and I think: If only I could *begin* to explain.

Soon after breakfast I find myself standing in Tony's room, smaller than my own, skimming my fingers along the spines on his bookshelf, picking up and setting down his keepsakes: a letter opener Vicky brought him from Kenya last year, a jokey snowstorm paperweight containing a miniature snowplow. His guitar, a Fender Strat clone, leans against one wall. I pick it up, try a couple of chords, but it sounds out of tune and I soon put it back where it came from. What I'm doing here exactly I really don't know. Ask me another. Lolling on the foot of his unslept-in bed, I put on his Sennheiser headphones and push a convenient CD into his player, something from the late eighties by The Pixies. It isn't exactly restful, like many of the things Tony listens to these days, so after a minute or two I reach for the player and turn it off, then sit there in the whistling silence that follows with the phones still on, thinking absently Bob Clark, must see Bob Clark, must see Bob Clark right away.

I'm still reciting this to myself as, casting aside the phones, I curl up on Tony's bed and close my eyes. Must see . . . must see Bob Clark. When I wake two hours later to the sound of Sunday-morning lawnmowers and radios, I'm feeling rested and calm and ready to go again, and most of all relieved because for once, even though I've just slept like a log, I don't remember dreaming at all.

14 TONY

Can't hear ... can't see my hand in front of my face ... can't even think ... It takes about twenty minutes before I calm myself down. I count the seconds in each minute, and reaching sixty begin again. You could go mad like this very easily. Wait till I get my hands on him, just wait; but then what?

My watch isn't luminous; I can't even hear it ticking. Soon I lose track of the hour. All I know is that the alarm is set for eight in the morning and there's an eternity to go before that.

What has he done, this brother of mine? He has finally flipped, that's what, but does *he* realize it? Maybe I should have seen it coming—or maybe I did, but couldn't believe he'd go through with it. After the door shuts in my face, there's a silence that goes on and on. I don't hear his footsteps leaving the cellar, but it's hard to imagine him still standing there near the door, listening. It probably means the walls of the storage room are too thick to hear through; either that or the beat of my heart between my ears drowns everything out.

"Joke's over," I call to him hopefully. "Let's just say this never happened."

After a while I sit down—slide to the floor, my back pressing the door—and try to think. In time I'm breathing more steadily and can tell that the thumping between my ears is actually the pulse beat of the party upstairs, though I can't hear voices—laughter, small talk—and have no reason to believe they'll hear mine. All the same I'm near to screaming, making as much noise as I can, because at the back of my mind I'm thinking suppose he doesn't come back tonight? Suppose he never comes back at all?

What I can't afford is to let myself panic. I've got to stay in control. Now that this has happened, the only thing to do is imagine a way out. Leaning back against the door, I screw my eyes shut and try to focus my thoughts. Right away I see a tent in a field, early morning, with the sun just coming up; this is years ago. Outside the tent is a portable gas burner with a small aluminum kettle on top that is steaming and whistling. Squatting beside it, Keith Dent is preparing breakfast, opening a can of baked beans with a Swiss Army knife. I'm just getting up, rubbing the sleep from my eyes, nursing my aching neck and shoulders. This is shortly after my thirteenth birthday. It's my first morning camping and I'm slightly clueless about how to survive in nature with so few luxuries. For one thing, it's the first time I've slept without a pillow. Fumbling my way clear of the tent, I'm carrying a towel and a washcloth and a bar of white soap, and all I can see are fields and meadows, grazing cattle.

"Morning," Keith Dent says brightly. "Sleep well?"

"Oh, sure. What's the time?"

"Never mind the time," he goes. "That's why we're here. To forget stuff like that for a while."

It was Keith's idea that we borrow his dad's tent for the weekend, and my dad who drove us to the country, all the time reminding us that we were only a phone call from home if we needed anything: our safety net. After he'd dropped us and we'd started to pitch the tent, Keith said to me, "You even *think* about calling and I'll strangle you."

Even then I didn't quite get the point. Watching him open the beans, I ask hopefully, "Where's the bathroom? Is there a shower room round here somewhere?"

Keith shakes his head stiffly, makes a clucking sound with his tongue. "Come here," he says, indicating a spot some distance down the hill across the meadow. "See those trees? There's a stream running between them; you can't really see it from here, but you'll hear it when everything's quiet. That's your shower room, *and* your bathroom."

Fifteen minutes later, stripping off my clothes at the water's edge and dipping into the cool, clear running water, I begin to feel—not embarrassed but strangely alive, excited, free. Last night while reading by flashlight after Keith fell asleep, a snoring heap in his sleeping bag, I kept breaking off to wonder what I must be missing on TV. Then I started to think about the telephone booth about half a mile along the main road from here. Should I call home to let everyone know how I am? Suppose they're worried? Yet this morning, by the time I'm towel dried and sitting cross-legged at the tent, eating beans from a noisy tin plate like John Wayne, I don't want to phone and I really don't give a damn what's showing on television.

Later, as we're loading our backpacks and rolling up the tent before moving on, Keith Dent tells me, "Survival, that's what this is about. You can run home to Mommy anytime you like, but the point is one day she won't be there to run home to, you'll be on your own with no one to rely on except yourself. Know something, Tony? First thing I'm going to do when we get home tomorrow is stash my stuff in the washing machine, run a nice hot tub, and soak in it for an hour or so, then put up my feet with a microwave TV dinner and watch a good video or two. But as long as I'm here, I want to forget it; I don't want to have to rely on it. Maybe one day, who knows, we'll *have* to go back to the wilds, and then we'll just have to see who survives."

Why on earth this comes to mind as I sit cramped in the cool, moist storeroom in the cellar, I don't know; or perhaps I do. Perhaps what I learned from Keith is just this: that you have to make the most of whatever you've got, whatever you're born with, the hand you're dealt. I mean, let's face it, the hand Nick dealt *me* tonight really stinks, but it's all I've got. So I'm locked in this storage room; what else is there to do except make use of whatever is stored here?

The first thing, I figure, is to stand up, not sit; then to find the light, if there is one, and see whether it works. After a minute's fumbling, I locate the switch to the right of the door, but there's no response when I click it. So I stand with my back to the wall trying to keep calm to get some sense of the room I'm in. My breathing sounds sort of closed in, which gives me the feeling the storage room is small. Turning, following the wall to my right with both hands, I try skirting along, past the door, until the wall meets another in a corner where something solid and knee high blocks my path.

It feels like a packing crate, the kind they generally use for fruits and vegetables. It's loaded with papers—books or newspapers or something—that must have been down here a good while, as they're soft and damp to the touch. A little farther along, now moving to the left, something large and heavy and wooden stops me. It's a shelving unit, a free-standing bookshelf, and as my shoulder jars against it, something topples and smashes, smashes with a thin, glassy sound that makes me jump and cry out.

No one hears, no one cares. The party thump-thumps away upstairs regardless. Running my hands along the shelves, the first thing I come across is dust, and lots of it. Not only does it coat my hands, but it quickly fills the air, so that I sneeze three or four times, harder and more violently each time, which only raises more dust.

But there's more than grime on these shelves. A quick examination and I've laid claim to a claw hammer, a can of nails, and something that feels like an old toothbrush that I toss aside with a shudder. There isn't much use I can put the hammer and nails to, but finding them encourages me: There must be something useful stored here, not only moldering trash. Then—bingo—I skim my fingers across a small compact matchbox, which clatters when I shake it. Really, I can't believe my luck.

Already I'm grateful for those weekends spent camping, learning about survival, because otherwise I'd never appreciate such small mercies.

The only thing is—and this worries me even as I nudge open the matchbox—everything here has been down in the cool, moist atmosphere so long, the matches could well be useless. The first one I try does spark, though it doesn't ignite: The faintest click on the floor between my feet tells me the match head has split and dropped off.

At least it was alive, though. At least that's something. So I drag out another and scrape it, more carefully this time, down the side of the box. Nothing happens at all, even when I repeat this a second time, a third. With a forefinger I test the match head to make sure I'm trying to strike the right end: I am, but it's spent. Someone has replaced the damn thing in its box after use. Nick, you're to blame for this, for everything. Brothers are not *supposed* to act like you've acted.

All right, what I did, taking advantage of Alex, was selfish and out of line; partly it was because I didn't know how else to deal with a tough situation, but it's easy to see why he'd take offense. Even so, isn't this the wrong way to solve our problem? If we do have a problem, shouldn't we talk it out, sensibly and reasonably, brother to brother, before I wring his lousy neck?

Selecting a new match, I swipe it along the box edge. This time, third time lucky, it sparks, and the flame blooms up in the dark, so sudden and bright I'm forced to narrow my eyes to see. Everything around me is thrown into sharp relief: the bare brick walls, the rubbish stuffed into bags and crates, the shelves I'm stand-

ing in front of. Everything sways nearer and farther,
darker and lighter; shadows crawl up the walls as I cup
the flame in my hands. The last thing I notice before
the match burns so low I have to shake it out before
burning myself is a squat knob of candle, melted down
to the quick, on one of the shelves. I strike a new match
and light what's left of it—and it's then that I see the
two spare unused candles lying on the shelf beside it.
Not that there's much else to be grateful for down here,
but I'm grateful for the light. Catching my breath, the
flame flickers a little, and more shadows dip and dance
about the walls.

At my feet is another crate piled high with newspapers, many of them dated last year. Left here, I guess,
by the previous occupants. These aren't so damp or
musty as the first batch, so I unload and arrange them
crumpled in a corner near the door, where I can sit a
little more comfortably than on the bare concrete floor.

From the first box I pluck out a few of the less grungy
paperback novels and flop down with them, giving myself something to do. The important thing is to keep
my mind occupied; not brood or despair, even though
the candlelight isn't easy to read by. The first book is
a science-fiction novel, *A Scanner Darkly* by Philip K.
Dick, with a weird illustration of a large piercing
eye—nothing else—on the cover. The second is *The
Strange Case of Dr. Jekyll and Mr. Hyde*, which I've never
read. Also there's a fantasy title I've never heard of before: *Deuce* by Robert Knight. The cover is two crossed
swords, sparks flying as they collide, with a misty sort of
background of distant castles and mountains, smoke and
flames. Reading the blurb on the back of this one, I

nearly gag in amazement. It's either the book Alex described at the coffee shop today or else one very much
like it. A lifelong feud between all-powerful twin brothers threatens to destroy both their kingdoms, Western
civilization, the world, you name it. Even though I didn't
get Alex's last name, I'm fairly sure this is her father's
work. It's a novel, though, not an adventure-game book,
and after the title page there's a dedication that leaves
me in no doubt at all:

> *To my daughters with love—*
> *Alex, my greatest fan and sternest critic;*
> *and Claire and Denise,*
> *who inspired this tale without knowing it*

Suddenly, God knows why, I have an uncontrollable
urge to start reading. It's more than to pass the time,
though; it's to learn something—maybe even something
about *us*, me and Nick. There's no such thing as coincidence, I tell myself, turning to the page where the story
begins. There's fate and there's destiny but no coincidence. Everything happens for a reason, has to, no two
ways about it. What else am I supposed to believe when
the blurb on the back of the book reads *For years the
brothers waged war—and all because of a terrible misunderstanding*?

So I begin to read, forgetting where I am, forgetting
the time. When the squat, used candle begins to burn
down, I light another and continue, not even thinking
of crying for help or puzzling my way out, not thinking
of anything except the two brothers in the story because
I desperately need to know one thing: *What* misunderstanding? Where did they go wrong? And were they
ever able to put it right again?

15 NICK

It's another hot, bright afternoon, and on St. Dominic's Square a group of kids are arguing over who's pitching, who's batting. You can tell right away that the older boys (two from my class who I don't really know) have taken over the game, and now the youngsters are getting agitated. One of them picks up a stone and threatens to hurl it. "Put that down or I'll kill you," says one from my class. "I'm not playing with *you*," says the kid, who then drops the stone and pockets the ball instead.

Games, who needs them? I'm thinking. Is there any such thing as a *game* anymore? Does anyone play fair?

Now the kid from my class (Mark Fletcher is his name) is striding up to the smaller kid and wrestling the ball from the kid's pocket and twisting the kid's arm up behind his back until he cries out and hands the ball over. There are insults flying back and forth, and the smaller kids are all backing off, picking up stones of their own.

Somewhere in the distance you can hear dogs barking at each other across developments and mothers screaming at their children to come here, go away, stay there. Maybe it's the heat, I'm thinking. It reaches a certain level and stays there for so long, so hot and humid, and all at once everyone's temper starts to fray and then people do things they . . .

People do things they regret.

Bob Clark, I'm thinking. Must see Bob Clark. Tony *pushed* me, I didn't fall. He can't blame me for everything. All this stuff has been racing around in my head for hours, so no wonder I couldn't sleep in the night. Physically I feel better for the hour or two on Tony's bed this morning, but in every other way I'm restless as hell.

Fortunately, the first thing I see when I get to Bob's house farther down the block is Bob himself, washing down his dad's car. Parked on the driveway is a pickup truck with a mountain of builder's materials—copper pipes, insulated wiring, bags of cement—in the back. There's a bucket at Bob's feet, and he's smearing a large, soapy sponge all over the car's roof and hood while the radio inside plays reggae: Augustus Pablo. He's wearing only swimming shorts and sneakers, and his arms and shoulders have a deep-red, shiny, sunburned look. Seeing me, he sort of grins and winks, not stopping what he's doing.

"How's tricks, Nick? Where're you going—to meet the girl of your dreams again? Har har."

"Not yet," I go, leaning against the driver's side door.

"Off the paintwork," he says. "My dad'll kill you. Well, no: He'll kill *me*. You're just visiting. *I'll* kill you."

"Everyone's threatening to kill everyone today. Why is that, do you think? The heat?"

"What?" he goes, not looking up.

"As a matter of fact, I came to see you."

"Well, I'm honored. Don't tell me: You want me to be best man at the wedding." Seeing my expression, he stops for a moment and says, "You and her, I mean. You were pretty well practically *engaged* last night, weren't you? At the gig, I mean, and the party afterward. Had to avert my *eyes*, you know."

Instead of rising to the bait, I count slowly to ten while he dunks the sponge in the bucket, squeezes it out, moves back and forth across the hood, the suds draining away down the gutter.

"So, what did you come to see me about?" he wants to know. "Or is it that you just can't resist my winning personality?"

"Sure I can resist. Do you think I'd come near you just for *you*?" He feigns a punch at my head, and I feign being hit. "Actually," I go, "I *did* want something. I need helping out."

"Really? How?"

"It's about me and Alex." He glances up from his work with interest. "We'd like to have some time by ourselves—"

"So I'll stay out of your way. No problem."

"That's not what I mean, dope." I'm pocketing my hands now, watching my sneakers and fidgeting, not meeting his gaze, because this is all a bold lie and faintly embarrassing. Agitated, I tug at the collar of my navy Fred Perry shirt. Is it hot or is it hot? "What I mean is, we don't have anywhere to go, not on a Sunday. The town's all closed up and everyone's at home—my folks are doing some barbecue for their friends and Alex is staying with her cousin. We'd like to spend some time together, but . . ." I trail off, hoping he'll complete the picture for himself.

But the airhead throws up his hands in innocence, spraying a thin trail of suds across the street. "So what do you want me to do? Why don't you take her for a walk? There's fields—there's a park just a bus ride away."

"Everyone goes there on Sunday," I tell him. "Families. Screaming kids. Grandmothers. Dogs. Ice-cream salesmen. We wouldn't have a minute's peace."

"Hmmm, I can see that." Bob's grin is broad and mocking because he knows exactly what I'm asking for but prefers to make me suffer for it. "So if I help you out, what's it worth?"

"I'll do your math homework next term."

"No thanks. You're even worse at math than I am. But if you can get your brother to do it . . ." Still beaming, he drops the sponge in the bucket and wipes his hands on his shorts. "Let's just say you owe me one. Won't be a minute; wait there."

With that, he turns and runs up the driveway and around the side of the house to the back. I stand in the street, trying to collect my senses in the heat, taking deep breaths, but there's very little air and my head is swimming. After a minute or two the Augustus Pablo track on the radio fades and a DJ's voice breezes away about this and that before some oldie—"No Woman No Cry"—starts up. I'm just getting lost in the music when Bob returns, waggling the sliver of steel key in my face.

"This is for the back door," he says very soberly. "The front one's on a Yale, and there's no key for that, so if you open it from inside, you'll have to make sure the latch is dropped when you leave." He hands it over and I stuff it deep inside a pocket, where it clinks against the key, which I took from the cellar door. "It's the only copy, so take care of it, and remember: My dad doesn't know a thing. If word gets back to him about this or the parties, he'll *liquidate* me, understand?"

I nod. "All we want is a little time to ourselves. This is just between you and me."

"Dead right." He checks over his shoulder—no sign of his father—and relaxes again, returning to washing the car. "You won't find it very comfortable though. You've seen for yourself. There's nothing on the floors and no chairs or anything."

"We'll manage."

"Har har. I bet you will."

"Sure we will," I go. "And I'll get this key back to you soon as I can."

"No hurry. Anytime in the week's okay with me. Just be careful. And remember to practice safe sex."

"Of course," I go, and laugh. But, walking away, I'm thinking: The mentality of some people, my *God.*

16 TONY

After a while the smell of the burning candle in the small dark space becomes overpowering, and I wonder whether I should snuff it out and leave the rest of Alex's father's book for another time. Marking my place about halfway through, I shift onto my side and check my watch—six A.M.: unbelievable. The party must've been over hours ago. Since midnight I've been reading, napping, tossing and turning on a bed of old newspaper, cursing my luck and my brother, all the while growing hotter and weaker as the cellar begins to seem less cool.

A few hours ago everything seemed very different: I'd wait out the storm, wait until Nick or someone came for me, which I was fairly certain they would. But now I'm not so confident.

At the point where I've marked my place in *Deuce,* the two brothers are now separated and one has declared war on the other, which doesn't bode well. After

all they've been through, and bearing in mind the differences between them, it's hard to imagine them ever
making up. Their problems begin with their upbring-
ing: In their seventh year one of the brothers (By-sor)
is stricken with a rare illness that means he has to be
quarantined for nine months. One of the side effects
of the illness (a sort of amalgam of malaria and coma)
combined with separation from the world is that he hal-
lucinates—dreams he is out of his body, watching over
the rest of his family, particularly his twin brother (Norvak), who is plotting against him.

His mother and father are wealthy lords of a land
called Byzantium, and in the dream Norvak is using
the supernatural powers he was born with (it's a sort
of involved story) to influence his parents, secure his
inheritance, and By-sor's share too. He wants the whole
kingdom for himself when his parents die, and this is
his chance to secure it.

Nothing of the sort is really happening, of course.
The kid in the coma is imagining, dreaming. But he
gets this unshakable paranoid idea into his head, and
even after he's fully recovered, he sees everything as
part of the same conspiracy: Everyone, but *everyone* is
against him. His mother's tears of joy, the way she hugs
him, his brother Norvak's cheers when By-sor finally
wakes from his coma in good health, the celebration
feast his father throws—all this is a mask to disguise the
fact they're against him. And this is where the war really
starts. For the rest of his childhood By-sor persecutes
Norvak. He tries to drive his brother either insane or
toward suicide, convinced this is the only way to save

his own share of the inheritance. Then the parents are tragically killed in an ice storm and a will is uncovered—a will they have recently changed because of the feud between the sons. The kingdom is to be split in two, half to each brother, who must spend the rest of their lives on opposite sides of Byzantium.

The tragedy, really, is that no one was ever plotting against anyone. Norvak's hands are clean, but tell that to By-sor! So from opposite poles of their land the feud continues. By-sor declares war on Norvak, and the powers they were born with (powers to destroy and read minds) are let loose in full force.

Strangely—or maybe not so strangely after all—this reminds me very much of a dream I have sometimes: a dream of myself and Nick, before we were born. It came back to me again in the night as I fell asleep over the book, between chapters, and for some reason it seems to make more sense this time than before.

In the dream, it is always the same. Our mother is on the main street, laden with shopping, when she feels a sharp kick inside, a kick violent enough to cause her to drop both her bags outside Woolworth. She steadies herself in the doorway, takes several deep breaths. After a moment she pats her stomach and smiles and says, "There now, there now. That's enough of that. . . . No squabbling, you two."

If only she knew, though. If only she had half an *idea*. Inside our mother, Nick is watching me closely while I sleep, which means I can sleep only in fits and starts. Who could *rest* in a weird scene like this? He's sizing me up—God knows what for—and when I wake he sort of spits under his breath, "You think you're really some-thing, don't you? You think you're number one, her pride and joy."

At this point I've only just woken, a little disoriented, and I haven't a clue what he's ranting about.

"You're not going first and that's that," he goes. "If I let you go first, they'll always look down on me, I'll al-ways be second in everything."

"Don't be crazy," I tell him. "Once we're out there in the world—well, anything can happen, really anything. We won't be enemies, we'll be brothers, friends. We'll be equal and we'll both make the best of what we've got."

"No we won't. Because there won't be enough of any-thing to go round. There won't be enough intelligence or love or anything. One of us will have to finish first. Survival of the fittest. *Comprende?*"

I take a long moment to think about this. "But when the time comes, there'll be nothing we can do. We'll have no choice about being born. We can't choose who goes first, for crying out loud. If it happens to be me when the time comes—"

"It won't. Because I won't allow it." This is spoken so harshly, the only thing that's lacking is a special-effects department: a double clap of thunder, a dancing strobe of lightning. My mouth runs dry just listening to him.

"Nick, we're brothers," I go. "We've shared everything so far, haven't we? Our mother's blood, the air she breathes. If we can share so much now, what's wrong with later on?"

He's about to reply when a sudden crunching, split-

ting sound overhead wakes me up. I'm jolted out of the
dream, which is still clear as crystal in my mind, and I'm
back in the cellar again. The candle is much lower than
the last time I looked at it, and I must have slept through
the alarm because my watch says five before one. My
body is just one mass of aches and my head is thumping.
I'm hungry and alone and on the verge of screaming
out, even though no one will hear me.

But then it comes again—the noise that woke me,
which I now realize is a crunching and splitting of wood
somewhere overhead. Gazing up through the gloom to
the ceiling, it's hard to actually see anything, but the
sound is up there, directly above me, no question.
There's a thump, a clatter (footsteps; a heavy tool being
put down, picked up) and the splintering starts over
again. What day is it? Sunday? Monday? Are new occupants moving in? Can't think. Doesn't matter. Must find
my voice. Must make them hear me.

My heart almost choking me, I manage to cry out.
"You up there! Help! Hey you!"

No one returns my shout, but the noise continues.
Have they heard me, or has the noise they're making
drowned me out? They're above me, though, tearing
up a floorboard to get at me.

"Down here!" I go, louder. "Right below you in the
cellar! Can you hear me? Can you hear—"

"I can hear you," he goes, and my heart sort of leaps
and sinks all at once as I recognize the voice, and the
floorboard comes up and the narrow band of light appears above me, straight and narrow and harsh as a
fluorescent bulb going on. Covering my eyes with my

hands, I manage to peer between my fingers, and it's then that I'm able to see Nick leering down at me, still clutching the hammer or chisel he's used to break through.

"Tony?" he goes. "You all right?"

After everything I've been through, it's hard to hold back. "What do you *think*? What do you bloody well *think*!"

"There there," he says softly. "There there. I came back to see you, didn't I?"

"That's not half enough. You're not even warm. Do you know what it's like down here, no food, no drink, no air, no one knowing?"

"*I* know, Tony. *I* know you're there."

"That's such a great help. You have no idea what a load off my mind that is."

There's a silence then. I can't see his face exactly, though I can sense he's turning things over in his mind. At last he says, "Here, I brought something for you. I brought you something to eat and drink."

He raises a hand, and something dark and fast comes flashing down from above. I catch the missile—a rustling plastic bag weighted with sandwiches or something. I look up and a second missile—this time a plastic bottle—swoops down.

"Peace offering," says Nick, and clears his throat. "Something to keep you going."

"Peace offering?" I can hardly believe what I'm hearing. "You think I'm going to forget this?"

"Last night you weren't playing that tune. Last night it was Let's forget this ever happened, Nick; no hard feelings, Nick; joke's over. Remember?"

"So . . . so what are you planning to do? Keep me down here?"

"That depends."

"On what?"

"On you."

Again there's a silence. Above me Nick's silhouette is absolutely still, unreadable. Something snapped, I'm thinking. Something snapped in his brain. Calm yourself, play along with him. Keep your head or he'll punish you for it. I take a moment to unscrew the cap from the bottle he threw me and take a long, parched swallow. The bottle contains water that tastes faintly of plastic.

"So what do I have to do?" I ask him.

"Just quit," he says. "Just quit what you've been doing. Taking everything away from me."

"Alex, you mean? Okay, you can have her. She's yours. Look, I just lost my head for a minute, and who wouldn't? I was swept off my feet, that's all. But no wonder. She's terrific. Just terrific. As a matter of fact"—I'm croaking, and reach for the bottle again—"as a matter of fact, what choice do I have but to come clean with her? You wouldn't believe how hard it was, all the time I was seeing her, thinking about Vicky, trying to figure how to explain . . ."

"This isn't the first time you've done this to me. You played the same game with Vicky too. Everything I ever wanted you've taken for yourself."

"Really, Nick, I wouldn't—I never—it may look like that to you, but I never meant things to turn out the way they did. When I met Vicky—"

"I'd told you about Vicky," he snaps. "Took you into my confidence. The only time I ever really did. Poured

my damn heart out about her. Remember the night we
sat in your room and I told you how I felt, how I wanted
to ask her out but was afraid? And you told me you'd
see what you could do? You'd have a quiet word with
her? You always had a way with words when it came to
girls. You weren't fazed at all."

"Well, that's right . . ."

"It's *damn* right where Vicky's concerned. I don't know
what you told her, but she never looked twice at me
again. Next time I laid eyes on her, she was clinging to
your arm, you slime bag."

Jesus, I'm thinking. Whatever I tell him, he's going
to suck it in and spit it right back at me. He doesn't want
to know or believe I never meant things to turn out like
this. He has his own talents and I have mine, and what
happened with Vicky—and again with Alex—was acci-
dental, unplanned. I shake my head, no longer angry
with Nick, just wishing I could reach him somehow,
make him see.

"When I spoke to Vicky," I tell him, "I realized right
away she was interested in me. It was like—" Oh God,
how can I say this? "Like an understanding we had right
from the start. We clicked, and I knew it, and she wasn't
confused by the fact we looked alike, you and me, she
seemed to know exactly what she wanted. . . ."

"You never told her how *I* felt, did you?"

"I'm sorry." Really, honestly I am. He won't believe it
for a moment, but it's true. "Things got out of hand."

"No kidding."

"It looks," I go quietly, "as though they got out of
hand again." Nick says nothing. "So what now? What

do I have to do? Do you want me to tell Alex what I did? How I misled her? I'll do it. You want to bring her here so I can explain?"

"No," he goes. "No, not that."

"Then will you let me out? Will you trust me?"

"Can I, though?"

"What else can you do?"

My neck is beginning to crick from the strain of staring up at him. For a moment I turn my attention to the food parcel, tearing it open, biting into the first of several hefty doorstop sandwiches, which almost chokes me as I swallow. Ham with lettuce. Too much mustard.

"You're my brother," he says vaguely after a while.

"Of course I am," I go. "What's that supposed to mean?"

"Just that you shouldn't have let this happen. You pushed me too far this time."

"But you overstepped the mark. You're way out of line, Nick."

"Don't think I'm not sorry. But you're never as innocent as you make yourself sound. You knew about Alex and me, you knew what you were doing."

"God help us," I mumble through a mouthful of sandwich. "Next you'll be telling me I'm out to get you! I've been plotting against you ever since—"

Suddenly I stop. The back-cover blurb of Alex's father's novel is trapped in the light from above. *For years the brothers waged war—and all because of a terrible misunderstanding,* it reads. It seems to make sense and yet doesn't. For a second I can almost feel my mind whirring, trying to fit several stray pieces together. Alex's rival twin sisters, the brothers in *Deuce,* this lunatic scene.

"Nick?" I say very softly. "What went wrong between us?"

He takes a long moment to consider. Then says, "Something did. Something went wrong."

"But suppose it didn't? Suppose nothing went wrong, but somehow we both grew up thinking it did?"

"What the hell are you talking about? Would you mind repeating that in some known language?"

"I've been reading this book," I tell him. "Never mind the whole story. The point is, it's about a misunderstanding, about the way we think other people see us. Nick, this book has two brothers, and one fears the other because he's convinced he's plotting against him. When he's not, you see, not really. . . . It's just that the first brother dreamed this was happening and . . ." I trail off there, thinking, Christ, this doesn't make sense.

"You've flipped," he goes. "Maybe that's what comes of being alone in the dark for so long."

"But listen, Nick. This is dead serious. The only reason I mention it is that the dream made me think about us." I wait. He's silent. I press on. "It's a dream I keep having. I dreamed it again last night. I remember it clearly. It's a dream I've been having for years."

"What dream?" There's a faint note of caution in his voice.

"About you and me. Before—well, before we were born."

"Don't—" he says sharply. Then, "Don't make me laugh."

"Shall I tell you what happens and what I think it means?" I ask.

"No, I'm not interested. I don't want to hear." After a pause he says, "Dreams don't mean anything anyway."

"Then let me tell you what I *think*. What I think is, you've always wanted to be more like me, Nick, and less like yourself. You want to be someone else."

"Total bull. Where did you dredge that idea up?"

"I'm serious. Listen." My voice is cracking. I can tell from his tone that this could be my last opportunity. Any second now he's going to stop listening, he's going to cover his ears to shut out the truth. "You wish you were more like me because you wish you had other talents—and I'm not just talking about girls—"

"That's crap and you know it. You're talking utter crap, like always."

"For God's sakes, this is important. Will you hear me out? Nick, what I learned from the book . . . even what I learned from just sitting here thinking it over . . . Shouldn't we be glad to be different? Isn't it great that you can run like the wind and I can play guitar and do well in class or whatever? Isn't that better than being the way our mom always wanted us to be? The same?"

He takes time out to think about this. Above me, his silhouette hardly stirs. "I want us to be different," he says quietly. "Do you?"

"Of course."

"Then why did you want to be me when you were with Alex?"

"I didn't—I swear—"

"You're a liar," he says. "As far as she's concerned, you *are* me."

Suddenly the air in the cellar is cold again, icy. For a time I feel that I'm drowning, that I never learned how to swim. My arms are rigid, my eyes are burning, and Nick can either let me go under or fish me out. The choice is all his.

"It's hard for us because we've always been so close," I tell him. "We always had to wear the same clothes, do the same things. Mom liked things that way; she didn't see what was happening. Even now she'd prefer to think there isn't any difference between us and we haven't grown apart. But we have different friends, we do different things. And what's wrong with that? Do we have to be enemies? What happened between us, Nick, to make us like this?"

"*You* know," he replies, and I think: Oh my God, full circle, we're back there again. He won't let it go. He doesn't want to take a step back and see how crazy this is. All he can see is Alex and me in each other's arms. He's that Staffordshire bull terrier shaking a rag, his jaws locked together, refusing to give in.

"Remember what you said just a minute ago?" I ask him. "You're my brother, you said. That matters. In the dream—"

"Not the dream again."

"Yes, the dream. About before we were born. We shared things then—that's what I learned just sitting here. We were inside our mother, the two of us, you and me together, arguing. But even though we were arguing, we were sharing everything."

"Sharing what?" he asks.

"Everything. The air, her blood, the whole damn thing. Just you and me sitting there in the darkness together. Brothers. You get me? How could anyone be any closer than we were?"

"Shut up!" he shouts, his voice so hard and hostile, it feels like another black missile coming down. "We didn't share anything. We weren't ever like that. How can you sit there after what you've done and pretend you ever shared any damn thing with me? You said *you* were going first when the time came. The dream was nothing like that. It was—"

Suddenly he stops and draws back from the hole in the darkness above me, at the same time slapping a hand across his mouth.

"Nick?" I go, but he doesn't reply. For a long time he just sort of wavers up there, hand on mouth, with this strange muffled sound coming from him. Good God, I'm thinking, he's crying. What *is* this?

"What were you saying, Nick?" I ask him. "You were about to say something important. What have you seen, Nick? What do you know?"

"I can't . . ." His reply is fragile as glass. You can hear the tears blocking his throat. "I'm sorry, Tony. I just can't . . ."

Then he draws back out of sight, and the blackness caves in again as he slaps the floorboard in place and there are three, four explosions overhead as he hammers the nails back in.

Then there's silence. It's deadly, quite deadly. Worse than before he came, because deep down I know he's still up there, crying, going over what he's done, probably thinking there's no way to undo it.

Jesus God. I'll forgive him, I'll try to forgive him, we *can* undo this mess together, I'm thinking. What else is there to do when things get so bad? But then I hear his unsteady steps on the ceiling over my head, his steps growing fainter.

"Nick!" I shout hopelessly, knowing that he won't hear me. "Nick, what did I say? What did I say?"

If he leaves after that, I don't hear him. Not because the cellar is soundproof, but because this time I'm crying too, hard and painful and long, and you wouldn't expect to hear anything above noises like that.

17 NICK

O nce he started on about the dream, I just had to
get out of there, couldn't make myself stay a second longer. All at once it was like this hot flush came
over me and the dizziness made me feel faint, and I
knew that if I didn't move quickly, I'd fall. I'd crash
down right on top of him and there we'd be, the two of
us holed up together just like in the dream he wouldn't
stop talking about. We'd be stuck there forever, because
no one would ever know and no one would come. We'd
waste away together down there, arguing, arguing, talking. My God.

How did he know, though? How could he dream what
I've dreamed? It was as if he were crawling around in my
head somewhere, as if he knew all my thoughts. After
I've nailed down the floorboard and locked the back
door, I begin to calm down and I start to think, maybe
he heard me talk in my sleep once. He heard my dream
and today he tried to use it against me.

Well, it won't work, brother. This time you've over-
done it. I came to make you a peace offering, but you
threw it right back in my face. I'm angry at him, but
still sad somehow, deep down. The truth is, I'm all
mixed up. That's what missing sleep does for you.

It takes me about half an hour to leave the development. It feels like longer. Every few paces I have to stop,
turn, and look back until finally the house is well out of
sight. From the outside it could well be any old house—
you wouldn't think there was anyone inside or anything
unusual about it. There it stands near the end of the
row, with the fields behind it all yellow and sunlit, and
today everything seems very peaceful down there. Just
before I reach the main street above the development,
I slow down once again and tell myself: You've got to
stop worrying over him. First sort yourself out, *then* take
care of him. The strangest thing though. As long as
Tony was out and about, running free, before this happened, I just couldn't think straight, couldn't seem to
get my own life in order. Now that he's out of the way,
I can't think of anything but *him.* It's even worse than
before.

You wouldn't believe it, but just as I'm turning onto
the main street I spot Alex. At first she doesn't notice
me. She's wearing black jeans and this baggy bright-
yellow T-shirt with a picture of a handgun on it and the
words: "New York—It Ain't Kansas." Her hair looks
freshly washed and catches the light, seeming to shim-
mer. Then she sees me, puts up a hand, comes running.

As soon as she sees me close up, she sort of falters in

her stride and gives me this anxious, narrow-eyed look that makes me quake.

"Hi, Nick," she says.

"Fancy seeing you."

"Yeah. We must stop meeting like this." She tries a smile that doesn't quite fit. "What have you been up to?"

"Oh, this and that. You?"

"Mmm. More or less the same." You can tell she's dying to say something else, but she's holding back. Then she goes, "That place you took me to in town yesterday is open."

"Which place is that?"

"That Italian place. Ferguson's."

"Ferdinand's?"

"That's it." Ten minutes later she gives me the same worried look again over coffee. We're seated at a table near the window with a view of the street between the rubber plants, an occasional car, the closed Sunday shops. "Nick, what's wrong?" she asks at last.

"Wrong? Nothing's wrong. What makes you say that?"

"Is it about me? Is there something . . . ?" She stops and stirs her coffee at length, not tasting it. "You've changed since yesterday. You're just like you were last night. Does it have something to do with me?"

"Not exactly."

"Then what? We can talk about it, whatever it is. I'd like us to talk, if you want to. What's up? Your eyes are so heavy and . . . Nick, have you been crying?"

"Don't be silly. Boys don't cry." I'm joking, but it

sounds very feeble, like a sort of admission. "It's nothing I can't sort out myself."

"Boys never like to talk about things either," she says. "They keep everything bottled up inside. They're afraid to talk. They rant about soccer and motorbikes instead. It's all a big stupid macho game."

"What do you want me to say?"

"Nothing, if that's how you'd like it. It's just that yesterday you were so easy to be with, so open and . . . loving." She fixes me with a gaze that makes me want to take her in my arms and scream at the same time. It's supposed to remind me of everything we shared last night. "And right now you're closed up like a clam. Didn't yesterday mean anything, Nick? Are you trying to push me away now?"

Suddenly the things she's saying and the way she's watching me make total, appalling sense. Something happened between Tony and her—you can tell as much from the glimmer in her eyes. She's in love with him; not with me, not with the one she thinks. There *is* a difference between Tony and me, a difference that has nothing to do with our looks, our clothes, or whether our hair is gelled up or brushed down. And while I sit there sipping my coffee, I realize that nothing I can say now will win her back. Whatever she's seen in Tony, it's something she wants, and even if I found her first, I have no claim on her. She's her own person. She'll go where she chooses with whoever she chooses—just the way Vicky did before her.

Before I can stop myself, it comes out. I've no way of stopping it. First there's this ache that fills my chest and throat, the back of my head, and then the tears are marking hot little trails down my cheeks.

Alex reaches for me, takes my hand, draws nearer. Thank goodness, I'm thinking, thank goodness this place is so empty. Across at the counter a blond waitress wipes dishes and pretends not to notice. There's a tape of Italian opera playing, and the waitress turns up the volume slightly. For a moment I feel oddly outside myself, a spectator watching the scene spin out. It's frankly embarrassing with me weeping and Alex clutching at me while the operatic music swells, like a scene in a corny film, *Brief Encounter* or something.

"Nick," says Alex. "There *is* something wrong. What's happened?"

"It's no good," I sniff. "You're right about what you said about boys never talking. There are some things you can't keep to yourself."

She gives my hand a gentle squeeze. "I'm here," she says. "Tell me."

"Yesterday wasn't everything you thought." Sniff. Sniff. "No matter how great it was or how much you loved it, it wasn't what you imagined."

"How's that?"

"This is hard, really hard."

"Take your time. That's okay."

"Remember when you asked me about my brother? The night we met? I told you he was nothing like me?"

She nods. "And yesterday when we were here, you didn't even want to discuss him."

"It's a very touchy subject."

"I thought as much." She's watching me so intently,

she doesn't even seem to blink. Through my tears she looks softly focused, touched here and there with strange dabs of light. "You told me his name was Tony, but that was all. To be honest, I thought—" She manages a smile. "Well, I got the feeling you were afraid I'd take an interest in him, so the less you told me the better. Didn't you know that's all it takes to make a girl curious?"

"I wish that was all there was to it." I'm forcing myself not to look at her now. On the street outside a flat-faced man with a barrel chest and huge muscly arms walks past with a rottweiler on a leash, and I absently wonder why it is so many dogs and their owners look so alike.

Alex squeezes my hand. "Well?" she says.

I take a deep breath. "Well, when I said he was nothing like me, I wasn't exactly telling the truth. In some ways he's a lot like me." Sniff.

"But you're not really close."

"No—in fact, we're at loggerheads a lot of the time. We just don't see eye to eye."

She nods. "You'd rather be at war than talk things through?"

"I guess. But that isn't the—that isn't what I'm trying to tell you."

She waits, calm and attentive. "Then what, Nick?"

"We're a *lot* alike, you understand? In some ways Tony and I are a lot alike."

A strange look comes over her. "What are you getting at?"

"Think about yesterday," I tell her after a pause. "Going to watch the sports and coming here and the gig and the party. Remember what a great time we had?"

Alex nods but says nothing.

Then I say, "Suppose I told you the great time you had was with Tony, not me."

It's clear she didn't expect to hear *that*. She looks stunned for a moment, as if I've just slapped her. Then she shakes her head slowly, resolutely, and says, "I wouldn't believe you, Nick."

"But it's true. The first time you saw me yesterday was last night at the party."

She laughs, but without a trace of humor. Her hand slackens its grip on mine. Then she looks away, clutches both sides of her head, and half laughs, half gasps. You can see the cogs turning behind Alex's eyes now; you can see all the things that haven't made sense before making sense now.

"Oh Jesus," she goes. "Oh my God. Oh my *God*." She slides back in her seat, calming herself, trying to regulate her breathing. "It was the party, you're right. That's where the change came over you. Oh my God. After your fall in the garden."

"Right. And I walked you home."

"And you didn't know where I lived."

"And when I kissed you, it wasn't the same for you."

I'm still sniffing back tears, and now Alex looks set to join me. Then, without warning, she lashes out at me, her flat palm striking me square on the left cheek. If the waitress sees any of this, I'm not really aware of it. All I can think of is the slow burning sensation down the side of my face.

"You bastards," she goes. "You've been making me feel . . . making me feel like . . . and all the time playing some stupid game with me. How dare you!" Her voice is raised, as keen as the slap she just gave me. "What do you think I *am*!"

"But it wasn't like that. It was—"

"Yes? Go on."

"It was Tony. I never knew he knew about you until I saw you together yesterday. You were right that I didn't want to tell you about him, didn't want you to find out anything about him, because I knew what he'd do. He's done it before."

"Done what?"

"Taken things away from me."

"Things? Am I just a *thing*?"

"You know what I mean."

She nods but says nothing. You can tell she still can't get her head around this. At last she says faintly, "Was Tony with me all day long then?"

"Up until the party, yes. The first I knew of it was when he had the nerve to bring you to watch me running. That was too much. I lost the damn race because of him."

Her face is set. She looks angry, muddled, confused. Her eyes seem to go away somewhere far distant, and I realize she's thinking about him, going over yesterday in her head. Then she looks at me squarely again.

"What happened at the party, Nick? Did you fight? Is that why you were in such a state, and you had to make up some story about falling down in the garden?"

"No, there wasn't a fight. Not exactly. I made him go away."

"So where is he now? That creep. That conniving bastard." But it's clear she still loves him really. "Where is he? Is he at home?"

"He's . . ." I stop, shrug, shake my head. There's the truth, and then there's the whole truth, and I'm unable to say anything more. Instead, I just sit there, twitching, nursing my stinging cheek, sniffing back tears. God, I'm thinking, what a mess I've made. What the hell do I do now? I have this slow, dreadful falling sensation, as if I'm poised on the edge of some cliff—the cliff in Cornwall all those years ago maybe—and about to go over. All I can see below me is blackness, the waves crashing over the rocks, the foam spraying up. And somewhere down there is Tony, crying for help, lost in the sea because I pushed him, and his cry makes me gasp and put both hands to my ears to shut out the sound. "Joke's over, Nick. Joke's over. Let's just say this never happened."

The next thing I know, Alex is getting up from the table, wiping her eyes with the heel of a hand. "Well?" she says. "Will I find him at home if I go there now?"

"Maybe," I go. "Who knows? I'm not his keeper. He has a girlfriend, you know. He could be out with her for all I know. What would you want to see him for after everything he's done?"

"I want to have this out with him. I want to let him know exactly what I think of him." She falters. "And I need to know if yesterday meant anything to him." She's making for the door of the coffee shop as she speaks. Before she goes out, she stops and gives me this sort of long, sorrowful look. "Nick, I'm sorry I hit you. You haven't done anything wrong. It wasn't you I meant to hurt. It was—"

"Tony?"

"Maybe." She shrugs. "Maybe both of you."

She's out the door before I can think of anything else to say. For a moment I wonder whether I might, somehow, be able to overtake her before she reaches our house; whether I might get there in time to become Tony—but the game playing is over. The joke is over. I don't have the strength to go through with that crap anymore.

18 TONY

19 NICK

"Nick? Is there something you aren't telling us?" My mother is pacing back and forth, wringing her hands together so violently you can hear the knuckles crack. Her breath sounds asthmatic, wheezing. I've never seen her like this before. But what can I do or say to stop her? Everything's out of control. I can't think, can't act. At the kitchen table, I pick up and put down a slice of toast from which I've taken one bite. Somewhere at the back of my mind a small quiet voice is screaming.

Across the table my father frowns and strokes his chin. "Didn't he say anything? That isn't like him. He would've at least left a message."

"Maybe he tried calling while we were out," I suggest.

"Maybe. But he'd have known we were here all weekend."

The panic is beginning to set in. You can taste it. It

colors the air. By Monday morning they're at that point where neither of them can stand still, where my mother seems constantly on the verge of tears. The sleepless nights are written across her face. I haven't slept either. The pressure is building inside me, like some bubble that's about to burst. My parents filed a missing persons report with the cops, and there was nothing I could say or do to stop them.

"You *would* tell us, Nick, wouldn't you, if you knew?" my mother says. The look on her face nearly kills me. "I mean, if Tony had some reason for going away that he didn't want us to know about . . . If he confided in you . . . If you felt you had to keep his secret—"

Which is about as much as I'm able to take. I scrape back my chair, struggle to my feet. "You think this is some kind of *pact*?" I yell at her. "Do you think if I knew I wouldn't say anything? Jesus, just look what this is doing to you." But I'm thinking: How can you do this, how can you lie to them? Yet every lie gives birth to another. "I know things are bad between Tony and me," I go on, "and they have been for so long, but does that give you the right to accuse me?"

My mother covers her face with a hand and half turns away from me.

"Calm down," my father says. "That's not what we're saying at all. No one's accusing you, Nick."

Dead right, I'm thinking. They think I'm upset for the same reasons they are. No one's accusing me of anything except myself.

■ ■ ■

And now Rees is on my case again. "Nicholas *Lloyd*," he's going. "Nicholas *Lloyd*! Are you here or somewhere else, lad?"

"Somewhere else," someone mutters behind me. "Cloud nine. Another time, another place."

"Why don't you wake up, Lloyd?" says Rees, and someone else, in a very low voice, says, "Why didn't you tell him that before the 1500?"

There are titters and snorts. Everyone seems to be watching me. Then I see the leering faces of Terry Mulligan and Bob Clark, who gives me a sly wink and touches his nose and says, "I guess *I* know why he's tired, sir."

These are my friends, I'm thinking. These are my friggin' *friends*. What on God's earth am I *doing* with them?

The only straight face is Vicky's. She's watching like the others, but not watching me. She seems to be studying a point just in front of me—the empty space where Tony usually sits. Vicky doesn't know about the police report yet; no one outside the family does. It's only a matter of time, however. Whenever I glance toward the classroom window, I'm half expecting to see police cars lined up outside.

"I'm calling the roll, Lloyd," Rees goes on. "Clearly, your brother is absent this morning. Am I to mark you absent as well?"

"Well, you're talking to me," I mumble. "What do you think you should do?"

"What did you say?"

"Yes, sir. I'm here. Real sorry about that."

More titters, more snorts. Bob Clark shakes his head, winks again. "Wear you out, did she?" he whispers, but who could be bothered to reply to that?

I could kill him, really I could. But my strength is sapping. All I want is to be able to catch up on the sleep I've been missing; just collapse in a warm and welcoming bed and drift off. Last night was a nightmare. Tossing and turning. Seeing only one thing. The house in Rosemount with Tony inside it. If only I could wind back the clock, I'm thinking. It was bad enough when he was around, but this—this is worse. He dominates everything now. Every face I look at has his superimposed on it, especially Vicky's. Though we haven't talked this morning, you can tell she's dying to. Her eyes are searching, questioning me. "What's wrong? Where is he?"—and then I remember Alex asking the same question, and look where *that* led.

"What's wrong, Lloyd?" asks Rees. "Have you any excuse for your behavior this morning? Staying up all night watching videos, is that it?"

"No, sir." I shake my head, resolute. "A virus, I think. Coming down with a virus. My brother's just the same, only worse." I cast a quick glance in Vicky's direction. "I'm feeling pretty—"

"Mulligan," he continues down the register, "Terry Mulligan."

And the classroom around me fades to gray.

For a while I feel I'm on the verge of passing out. I haven't eaten anything since yesterday morning, and my shoulders and limbs are all tight and cramped, perhaps from the race, perhaps from stress. While Rees goes on with the register, I feel for the keys in my pocket, wondering what I ought to take Tony for lunch. Keeping him out of the way, that's one thing. But starving him? No way. This is my brother, remember. He needs me. It isn't that underneath it all I really hate him or anything.

The lesson is half over before I remember I ought to at least seem to be concentrating. Rees has whipped out a copy of *The Strange Case of Dr. Jekyll and Mr. Hyde* by Robert Louis Stevenson and is reading selected extracts and asking what the book says about the human condition. Terry Mulligan replies that he once saw the movie—or one of the versions of the movie—but never sat through it all because it was in black and white. Then someone asks if he ever saw *An American Werewolf in London* and suddenly there's excitement in the class and everyone's talking at once about scenes in *that* movie, the scene where someone gets chased through the subway system, the scene where a victim is eaten alive in a movie theater, and Rees is growing blue in the face, all the while glaring at me as if it's *my* fault.

The next thing I know, I'm sitting in Miss Welles's art class, gazing blearily at the preliminary sketch for my painting, the one of the young man reflected in the mirror, his reflection grinning back at him. By now I'm beginning to feel almost queasy, and I'm wondering whether I really do have some kind of virus when Miss Welles sort of sneaks up behind me and says quietly, "Very dark, isn't it?"

"Dark?" I go, casting a glance toward the window.

"This thing you're drawing," she says. "Very moody.

Very dark. I quite like it so far. But what are you trying to say with this, Nick?"

"Say? I'm not sure I'm trying to say anything."

"Just something that came into your head, is it?"

"Sure. I suppose."

"Every picture has a meaning—even if you don't intend it to have, it's still there. There seems to be a lot in this picture you could talk about. You need to be more aware of what you're doing, I'd say."

Clutching my chin, I study the sketch more closely, feigning interest. "What strikes you as interesting about this?" I go.

"Let me see. Well, the reflection . . . the lookalike. You didn't happen to have your brother, Tony, in mind when you started this, did you?"

"I don't know. I don't think so. This just sort of came to me."

"Hmmm. Just a thought." Now she's resting her hand with its ringless wedding finger on the desk beside me, and I'm almost embarrassed by how near she is, what with the smell of her talc and her voice so low and close to my ear. "Doesn't something about it strike you as odd?" she asks after a time.

"Odd? In what way?"

"Perhaps it's what you intended. The boy who's looking into the mirror seems older than his reflection. He seems quite tired."

She's right, though it isn't something I've noticed until now. The face staring back—the boy's own reflection—looks almost wicked, the way he's smiling. But the boy looking into the mirror is haggard, worn out, like he's ill or suffering or in pain or something. After a moment's thought I pick up my pencil and add a few lines to the face in the mirror, making him older too. Now the two of them are alike, except that the one in the mirror is smiling.

"So it wasn't intentional," Miss Welles says at last.

"No, it was a mistake." I shrug. But long after she's moved on to someone else, I'm still staring, bewildered. For some reason the reflection in the mirror now looks, if anything, slightly too old, so I add a few wrinkles and lines to the other. It's as if they're draining one another, I'm thinking; wearing one another out for no reason.

Which is when it hits me—what I'm feeling, the hunger, the tiredness, the ache that seems to fill my whole body. I'm sure that this is exactly what Tony is feeling. We're going through the same thing—draining each other, tearing each other to pieces . . . for what?

He could be dying down there because of me. I can practically feel what he feels. And now I'm afraid for him as much as for me, and the face in the mirror seems to be screaming or grimacing in pain, not grinning. And I half imagine that if Tony cuts himself on something down there in the dark, then I'll bleed.

When the lunch bell goes, I'm first in line at the school cafeteria, buying two identical shrink-wrapped packs of sandwiches and two Diet Cokes. What I've done to him is too much—much worse than I realized—and I suddenly have no idea how to deal with it. Feed him, keep him alive, is all I can think of. I shouldn't have done what I did, but can I really afford to let him out?

My mind is spinning like a top as I lurch across the

school yard, which is packed with kids. Everyone seems happy, knowing the summer vacation is near; everyone has more life about them than me.

I'm halfway across the yard when Vicky appears beside me, nudging my arm, eyeing the cans and sandwiches with suspicion. When I stop and turn toward her, I get the weirdest sensation that the yard and the school are whirling around me, as though I'm riding a carousel.

"Hi, Nick. What's up?" Vicky forces a smile that fades rapidly. "Is everything all right? Why the rush?"

"Rush? No rush. I'm just . . ."

"You're very pale, and jumpy as a cat on hot bricks."

"It's just this thing that's going round, this bug," I tell her.

"The same thing that Tony has?"

"Yes. It must be the heat. In the heat, you get all these viruses breeding." Even as I speak I feel nauseous, exhausted.

"Is Tony very ill?"

"Not seriously ill, but he's confined to his bed."

"Are you going to see him?"

"Yeah, I thought I might take him lunch." Twitching the sandwiches at her, I start moving toward the school gates, but Vicky matches me stride for stride.

"Would it be all right if I came with you?" she goes. "Seeing him might set my mind at ease. Would you mind?"

"Mind? Not at all. But—" I'm struggling for excuses, anything to get her off my case. "There might not be time."

Vicky just looks at me blankly.

"Time to get there and back," I go on. "I was going to leg it. You wouldn't be able to keep up."

"So we'll take a bus."

"Yes, but . . ." It's as if my mind is overloading. Can't think straight. Can't function. Can hardly breathe. I'm fumbling, practically passing out from the strain. Then I say stupidly, "The problem is, this thing he has, it's contagious. In fact, they've put him in quarantine."

"What?" she shouts, her mouth a broad O. "Contagious? But you said you were suffering from it too!"

"I think I might be. The doctor said I was really okay for school."

"No kidding?"

"No kidding."

There's a pause. We walk several slow, silent steps toward the gates before Vicky pulls me up short, her face set like plaster. "Why don't you tell the truth, Nick? What's really wrong? Please don't ask me to believe all this nonsense about he's in quarantine and you're rushing home to feed him with sandwiches and Coke. The last time I spoke to him, he sounded just fine. Out with it. What's going on?"

"I can't explain now," I tell her. "He's not seriously ill, but you can't see him yet. But you will before long, believe me." She's staring at me in such a way—her face taut with concern, disbelief—that I can't hold her gaze and instead look ahead to the gates.

Standing there, just outside, waving, is Alex. She's the last one I need to set eyes on right now; it's as though someone has hammered yet another new nail in my coffin. My stomach feels tight as a drum, just as empty. At first I pretend not to see her, but the next thing she's waving more vigorously and shouting, her voice high and hard enough to carry above the noise in the yard.

"Nick! Hey, Nick! Over here!"

"Who's that?" Vicky frowns.

"Oh, no one. Just a girl I know."

She nods, and backs off a little. "Your lunch date, I guess. Nice looker, Nick. I approve. Can't you give her something a little more appetizing than stale school sandwiches, though? You won't sweep any girl off her feet like that." She half turns away, then turns back. "Just tell me this, Nick. What on earth's wrong between you and Tony?"

"Really, I wish I knew," I shrug.

"Send him my love anyway," she sighs. "Tell him I'll call him tonight."

After what feels like an age, she finally heads off across the yard toward the main entrance, where her friends stand watching and waiting for the lowdown. But I can't feel relief. No matter how many excuses I make or how many lies I make up, there'll always be someone else asking questions, watching me closely for signs of guilt. Alex is still waiting at the gates when I get there. She's dressed in all black and her face is funereal too—you can tell she's not happy. Despite all her waving and shouting, she doesn't have much to say until we've walked from the school as far as the busy main street, where we stand for a while, fidgeting, avoiding each other's eyes.

"Well?" she says after a time.

"Is that any way to say hello?" I reply.

She watches the traffic for a moment, then turns back to me. "Who was that girl, Nick?"

"Oh, no one. That was Vicky. Vicky Riley. Tony's girlfriend that I told you about."

"Oh." She sniffs. "Then Tony isn't at school today?"

"No."

"Does she know, then? Has she seen him?"

"Not since last week. She's been away for a few days." I'm stranded, I'm thinking. I'm wanting to let rip—take off toward Rosemount, to check that Tony's all right. But I swear I can't move. Everything seems designed to hold me back. A police car speeds by, siren wailing, and I jump, watching it into the distance, wondering whether it's heading where I have to head.

"He wasn't at home yesterday, when I called," Alex says. "Your parents said they hadn't seen him all day. Your dad says Tony's always like that. Independent."

"So he is. So what are you worried about?"

"Just this. No one seems to know where he is. And if you do, you're not telling. I tried phoning your house just now—no answer. If he's not at home and he's not at school, where is he?"

I shrug.

"Why are you carrying two packed lunches?"

"One is for you," I go, pushing a shrink-wrapped sandwich toward her.

She pushes it back so hard it disintegrates. "More of your bull. Don't ask me to believe *that*, Nick. I wasn't born yesterday."

"Then don't ask me to explain anything now," I tell her, practically plead with her. This is Vicky all over again, I'm thinking. Tony's down there, trapped and suffering, and I can't get away. She's studying me closely again, her eyes slightly narrowed, and perhaps it's just that I can't disguise what I'm feeling anymore, the guilt I'm feeling, because she backs away from me with an expression that looks like sheer horror.

"My God," she says. "Something really *has* happened between you, hasn't it? Where is he, Nick? What have you—"

Her words are cut off by another siren: this time that of an ambulance giving chase to the cop car. When it fades, Alex says, "You're not making sense, Nick. Does that girlfriend of his know anything?"

"Vicky? Nah," I go, but it's too late to convince her, because Alex has seen something in my face—perhaps fear—and she's moving away from me, back toward the school. For a second I'm torn between stopping her, telling her everything, anything just to prevent her from going, and sprinting to Rosemount, where Tony is dying and needs me. Then all at once Alex is running, and I'm running too, but we're haring in opposite directions.

The town is crowded, the streets crammed with shoppers, and I'm dodging from side to side as I go, nearly knocking over a spray of flowers outside the florist's, nearly flooring an old gray lady with a walker. In the air there's the thick smell of smoke, and at first I can only think Tony, no, Jesus no. But the smoke can't be coming from the house in Rosemount; that's too far away to be so thick and so cloying.

The lights at a crossing take—seem to take—forever to change, and I really can't wait. I'm sprinting across the face of the traffic, ignoring the horns, sidestepping slower pedestrians until I notice the crowd bunching at a corner near the marketplace where the cop car and ambulance have drawn up. There's a biker's helmet lying in the gutter, and the biker himself is being hoisted onto a stretcher, his black leather clothing slicked with red. A short distance away there's a car—a white Mini Metro—with a dented side door and beside it the biker's Suzuki in flames. The sight of the accident, the damage, the blood, makes me run faster until the town is behind me and I'm pelting down the winding streets of Rosemount.

20 <u>TONY</u>

Slowly, it dawns on me: I must have been dreaming. I saw myself running toward the edge of something. It was as if I was winning a race of some kind, but when I looked back, there was no one else running, and all I could see was trees, huge and silent and still. Then everything seemed to slow down as I came within sight of the tape. I glanced down at my feet: for some reason I was wearing Nick's sneakers. And I felt the salty breeze in my face, raised my arms, broke the tape with my chest—and too late, saw the edge of what I was running toward. After that it was like any other dream of falling—the ground disappearing from under me, the rocks, the dashing black sea racing up. But, like always, before I hit bottom I woke.

I'm gasping for breath, trying to recover my senses after the shock. It takes me a while—I've lost track of time—to remember where I am. The candle—my last—must have burned out while I slept, and there's nothing but darkness again, darkness and no air and only the smell of dust and damp paper. My body is stiff with cold and I'm aching with hunger. After a while I force myself upward, both arms outstretched, and hobble through the dark until I can feel the shelves on my right, and feeling my way along these shelves, I fumble for the nearest wall.

Finally there's the cool, moist sensation of brickwork. I can feel the walls of the cellar spinning about me, making me dizzy. All I can do is just stand there, my palm pressed to the wall until the sensation passes. It's then that I notice the crack of light, fine as a pencil line, somewhere off to my left. I edge toward it until my knee collides with something bulky and solid. What I've stumbled across is a packing crate—two packing crates stacked one on top of the other. These are heavily laden with pots and jars that are slightly tacky to the touch. As I grasp the crate on top—a dead weight to lift that gives me an instant headache—splinters of wood dig into my fingers, the muscles of my arms and shoulders strain painfully. Once it's out of the way, I'm able to see more of the light, but the source is blocked by the other crate, which is heavier still. This one I have to drag, inch by inch, away from the wall until the shape it's been covering comes into view.

It looks like a kind of air vent, maybe eighteen inches by twelve, with a fine metal grille stretched across it. It's almost impossible to see anything through the grille, except for part of a garbage can and what looks like a pile of cement. As I crouch beside it, welcoming the flow of fresh air from outside, I begin to think of a scene in a film I once saw: the Incredible Shrinking Man holed up in a basement like this one, not yet small enough to crawl through the grille but still too small to make himself heard. For a while I crouch there and listen, and every now and then I hear voices in the street. If I can hear *them*, I'm thinking, they ought to hear *me*.

"Help me, someone, help me! Here, over here! Down here!"

The effort of screaming makes me feel empty, worn out. It takes me an age to get up the strength to shout out again.

"Help me, I'm trapped! Can anyone hear me? Please?"

This time there's a murmur of voices in the street—so near, so far. A dog begins barking. I listen and wait, my heart so hard in my throat, it makes me feel sick.

Then a man's voice goes, "Did you hear that? Someone shouting? Could've sworn they were crying for help." The dog barks again, then starts whining. "Where do you suppose it came from?"

"Search me," says the other, a voice I recognize—with a shudder—as Nick's.

"Help!" I'm going, panicking now, because it's flashing through my mind that if Nick wants to keep me here, he'll do anything to shut me up too. This man and his dog are my only chance. I must make them hear me. But my voice is feeble, there's no air in my chest, as if I've been running, and the more I cry out, the more feeble it sounds.

"Must've been mistaken," says the first voice.

"Sure," says Nick, who sounds closer now, maybe as

close as the front of the house. "That's probably what it was."

"Oh, well. 'Bye now," says the man.

"'Bye now."

Then everything happens so rapidly, steps thumping across the ceiling above my head. There's the slightest pause then—I'm staring up through the dark, expecting to see the floorboards torn back, but instead what I hear is the upstairs door, the one leading down to the cellar, and the crash of rusty bolts, first one, then another, and Nick's footsteps rushing down. My heart feels like a hammer thumping all through my body. As the door swings open I shuffle backward against the wall, blocking the vent, twisting myself around to face Nick. He's standing there in silhouette with a powerful light behind him, the light a hard yellow and dazzling to my eyes, and when he takes one cautious step inside the storage room, I can't think of anything except the race I won against him in Cornwall the time I pushed him over to get there first, and the dream I woke up from—the cliff top beckoning, the salty air in my face, and the fall . . . the endless fall down into blackness.

It's here, I'm thinking. I'm finally going to hit rock bottom, and be swallowed by the sea, never seen again, and at last Nick will have everything he's always wanted.

"Tony," he says.

"I'm here," I answer, weakly. I'm trembling now.

There's a long-drawn-out pause. The cellar revolves slowly around me. All I can hear is the slow, grating breath that he takes before saying:

"Oh Tony, thank God you're alive."

21 NICK

an't get my head around this—but after wanting him out of the way for so long, I'm almost faint with relief to see him alive, shielding his eyes from the light. Hearing him calling for help from outside was one thing; but this is almost too much. He's sort of crouched down against a wall at the far side of the storage room, and he has this startled expression, like a hare caught in someone's car headlights. Before I can stop myself, the words tumble out:

"Tony, thank God you're alive."

"Nick?" He sounds weak, but not angry at all. You'd think after everything I've done, he'd want to smash me to pieces. "Nick? What's happening?"

Until now I've had no idea what I was going to do when I saw him. I take a few steps farther into the room—then rush across and fall down on my knees beside him.

"It's over," I tell him, keeping my voice as calm as

possible, though I'm trembling all over. "I can't keep this going anymore."

He seems to relax, but shows no emotion. "I still hate you for this," he says quietly. "Chances are I'll always hate you for this."

"I know. Can't blame you. Chances are I'll still hate you too."

He laughs—more a wheeze, like a smoker's cough—and the next thing I know, I'm laughing with him.

"So you're letting me out?" he asks finally.

"I don't have much choice, do I? Do you think you can walk? Can I help you?"

"I think I can remember how to walk by myself. Just get me up on my feet. Christ, I'm numb all over." When I've finished helping him up, he says, "What were you trying to prove, Nick? Why did you do this?"

"Because," I begin, though I have to stop and consider for a moment. "I didn't know what else to do at the time. I went berserk, I guess, and then I couldn't figure how to untangle the mess. All I could think of was . . . I wanted you out of the way. Like I couldn't begin to live or think clearly until you weren't there anymore. I just lost control. And then, when I'd done what I wanted, I couldn't live or think at all!"

"We all go a little crazy now and again," agrees Tony. "You just went a little further than most."

After staying so long in the dark I'm amazed he can be so philosophical. "I thought you'd be furious, I thought you'd come at me with your fists flying."

"Frankly, I'd like to kill you," he goes. "But what

would that solve? We've gone on like this long enough, and I'm sick of it."

Together we move out through the storage room door, into the light in the cellar. "So what made you want to come back?" he asks.

"I don't know. I suppose—well, on the way over here, I kept thinking of that song by U2. 'I can't live with or without you.' Remember that one?" He nods and sort of smiles feebly. "All I wanted to do was put you out of my mind, and since Saturday night I haven't been able to think of anything *but* you. Remember when I was here yesterday and you mentioned your dream—the two of us arguing about who would go first, who would get born first?"

"I remember. It sent you into hysterics when I brought it up. You flipped out."

"That's because I dreamed the dream too. And what you said about all the things we shared, before we were born and afterward, it made me think about everything else we were sharing. I even got to feeling that if you stayed down here longer and died"—the word almost seals up my lips—"you'd take me with you. We'd both go together."

We're climbing the stairs from the basement as I tell him this. I've got his left arm slung around my shoulders and my right around his waist to support him, and before we reach the top he's grasping me more firmly, half hugging me.

"I'm sorry," I say under my breath, and Tony says, "Yeah. I'm sorry too."

It's as if something has changed in him while he's been down there, my prisoner. And something has changed in me too, though I really can't guess what or how.

"I've got a hell of a lot of explaining to do," I say as we enter the kitchen, where I've dumped the Cokes and sandwiches I brought him on the counter near the stove.

Tony slumps down on a chair at the table where Phil Mulligan and his cronies stood discussing crankshafts and pistons that night last week at the party, which now feels like months ago—years ago. "Me too," he goes. "We've both made a godawful mess of things. Have you seen Vicky or Alex?"

"Yes, but they both probably think I'm deranged or something. I could feel my nerves cracking when they asked me about you. Hadn't the foggiest idea what to tell them."

"You haven't told them anything, then?"

"Yesterday I sort of broke down and told Alex about how we were more alike than she could have guessed and how she'd been seeing both of us. But I never told her about any of this."

Tony manages a nod but sits slumped over the table, looking frail and pale. In fact he looks ready to faint. I slap the sandwiches and a Coke on the table, and he smiles and shakes his head and says, "Mmm. How nutritious. God, you're such a Philistine, Nick."

"This book you were reading," I begin, and pull up another chair, facing him. "The one about the twins at war with each other. Did you finish it?"

"Yes," he says flatly.

"How did it turn out in the end? What became of the brothers?"

"They destroyed one another in the end," he replies. Then, after a long awkward silence, "We've got to talk, Nick."

"We're talking now, aren't we?" Really, we haven't spoken like this in years, if ever before.

"I mean," he says, "we're going to have to get to the heart of this. Settle our differences. Work things out. Otherwise we'll be back where we were before all this happened. We'll just keep dragging each other down."

"I'll try," I tell him. I mean it, too.

"We'll both have to try," he agrees.

As he opens the can of Coke I've brought him—it almost explodes from the pressure—I hear the rise and fall of sirens. Tony takes no notice, but I'm sitting there rigid, my hands drawn into fists, for the sound brings back all the sensations of panic I felt as I ran toward town and smelled smoke from the burning Suzuki. I'm sitting there watching him drink from the can, thinking, somehow I've got to live with what I've done. People will eventually find out, and they'll think of me differently and look at me in a very new light, and I'll hate it, but somehow I'll have to live with that. Thank God he's alive though, I'm thinking. We can change. We will change. We'll both have to change. But at the same time the siren is growing louder, and something tells me—it's there in my bones—there's only one place that siren can be heading. Already they know what I've done. Already they're coming for me.

It's too soon for that. I need time and distance, time

to get everything clear in my head. And before I'm able to gather my senses I'm up on my feet, my chair skittering over on its side on the floor, and Tony is watching me, openmouthed.

"What are you doing, Nick? Now what's the matter?"

"The police. That's what. I can't—I don't want to—" All I can feel is this huge wave of guilt about what I've done, and the sudden desperate urge to be out of here.

"It's okay," he says. "It probably has nothing to do with us."

"Of course it has. All the houses on this street are empty. What else would they be doing down here?"

"So what? So what if they *are* coming here? Doesn't what we just talked about mean anything? What do you think they're about to do?—lock you up and throw away the key, for Chrissakes?"

"It's too soon," I tell him. "I just—I just need some time. I really can't handle this now."

"Okay, okay." Conceding, he puts up his hands. "So get moving. I'll explain everything. This is between you and me. None of their lousy business. And I'll see you later, at home maybe. We could invite Vicky and Alex? Lay *all* our cards on the table."

Even in my rush I have to marvel at his nerve, his cool and easy way of dealing with this. But I'm really not ready. Even if Tony forgives me—which is something else I can't get my head around—I haven't forgiven myself yet. There's so much to explain that I can't imagine how to explain. Later, I'm certain, I'll be fine. But now—

I'm on my way from the house as the police car prowls

down the street. I glance back behind me to see Tony standing at the door of the house, Coke can in hand. I stride briskly up the street, then break into a run. I'm not afraid, I'm thinking. I *will* be able to live with this because I'll have to, I'll have no choice.

Even as I run, thinking this, I feel lighter, stronger, and my limbs aren't constricted by cramps anymore. I'm free because Tony forgives me. I was the one with the jailer's key, but I was right there in prison with him, and he's let me out too. Somehow we'll work for an understanding. We won't destroy one another like the brothers in that book. And I'm lost in all that's happened today and since last week at the party as I run. I'm turning it all over in my head, I'm lost in my running, a picture at the back of my mind of a finish-line tape rushing toward me, rushing nearer and nearer, which is why I hardly notice the car speeding out from a junction on my right as I sprint into the street, straight into its path.

22 TONY

As soon as he starts up the street I *know* something dreadful's going to happen. It's almost as if—this is crazy, but it's really as if he's going all out to *make* something happen, to punish himself for what he's done before anyone else can.

It's all so confused and sudden that it doesn't seem real. First thing is that the police car comes rolling down the street, and Nick hits his stride as it reaches him. The car stops several houses short of the place where I'm standing, watching him go. The siren's still howling, but there doesn't seem any reason for it: The way the two cops look as they get out and stare up the street after Nick, you wouldn't guess there was any emergency. One of them glances over at me—I'm cowering in the doorway, one hand shielding my eyes from the light, which is very intense. Then he does a sort of double take and stares back up the street after Nick, who is now in full flow. You should see him run. The cops mutter a few words together and shrug, as if they don't know what to do. One of them then drops down into the car and gets on the radio while the other shouts after Nick— "Hey you! Hold it there!"

But Nick is bombing up the long, sloping street. You really should see him. It's something to behold. His head is tossed back and his arms move in lazy, graceful slow motion. His whole *body* seems to be moving in slow motion, except that he's really motoring, growing smaller by the second. The next moment the cop in the car who's on the radio turns the thing around with a screech of gears while the other one quits shouting and starts marching back down the street toward me.

And it's then that it happens. So far Nick has been running along the sidewalk, but now he cuts into the street. God knows what makes him sweep across the street without looking—but suddenly there's this car speeding out from the junction, not signaling, a silver-gray Rover as sleek as a gun, and as dangerous.

"Nick!" I scream out. "Nick! No! Please!"

There's a wail of brakes. The Rover swerves to a standstill. And in slow motion, still in slow motion, Nick is flying through the air like a stringless puppet, and there's a jolt in my stomach and chest that feels like a kind of explosion, and suddenly my legs are trying to buckle from under me. Nothing is real anymore. This must be a dream like the others. It must be a dream.

Just for a moment I'm on the edge of a faint. The daylight in my eyes is too harsh, all rainbow colors, and I feel myself falling, I hear the silence, I see the edge of the cliff and the blackness of rocks and sea below, and I blink and see Nick skidding across the street on his back. He doesn't move. He just lies there. I'm barely conscious, and all I can think of are his words just a few minutes back: If you stayed down here any longer and died, you'd take me with you. We'd both go together.

The cop car has pulled up beside him now. The other cop has forgotten me, and started back up the street. The driver of the Rover is out of his vehicle, pleading innocence. It's chaos from nowhere. And now I'm running too, running faster than I've run in my life before. There's another car at the junction now. The cop from the car is waving his arms for the driver to stop. Its doors fly open, and out clamber several faces I know: Bob Clark, and Vicky, and Alex. The driver is Terry Mulligan's brother, Phil. Vicky is screaming; or Alex; or both, I can't tell. There are neighbors from farther up the development running down to gawk at what's happened, and as I draw up beside Nick—there's blood on the road and his clothing is torn—all I want to do is bawl out the neighbors, throw something at them, make them go away, leave us alone. This is our damn business, I'm thinking. Go attend to your own.

I'm stooping over my brother now. One of the cops is trying to hold me back while the other is on the radio for an ambulance. I look up and see Vicky and Alex staggering forward, pale as ghosts, their features frozen; and then I look down at Nick again. His eyes are half closed; there's a thin trickle of blood from his right ear. But he's making a sound, a thin sort of rustling sound as if he's dragging for breath or trying to speak.

"Now look what you've made me do," he says faintly.

23 NICK

At the hospital in Wakefield they put me in a room of my own for the first few days until they're satisfied my condition is stable. Most of the time I'm drifting in and out of sleep, dreaming strange dreams. Then they ship me into a bed on one of the wards, where there's an old guy on my left who complains all the time to the staff when he isn't sneaking out for a cigarette, and on my right there's this kid about my age who spends all his time reading sci-fi books and won't talk at all, jumping a mile if you speak to him. He was admitted for an appendectomy, is the only thing I learn about him. The old guy claims there's nothing wrong with him and it's really just one big conspiracy to keep him here. One day I asked who was conspiring against him. Everyone, he said, just everyone. His family, the doctors, politicians. You name them. "Probably you as well," he said, and refused to answer my questions after that.

Me? There's a good deal of internal bruising, a fractured elbow, damage to the ligaments in my right hand and right foot that will probably take six or nine months to heal, they say. Which means I won't be running before next April; which could still give me time to be in shape to trounce Billy Mayhew in the 800 meters.

The visitors come and go at intervals. Many have signed the cast my right arm is set in. My parents fuss and worry, blame themselves, go through the same breast-beating routine every day during visiting hours. In the end I'm left feeling sort of sorry for them, because they haven't done anything wrong, even though they're convinced they must have. And the more of this I see, the more it comes home to me how many other people we affect when we go to war; how deeply we hurt them.

One fine morning Alex arrives with a card and a parcel. She's wearing white jeans and a raspberry T-shirt under a black cycle jacket. "The parcel's a copy of *Deuce*, the novel my dad wrote for my sisters," she tells me. "It's all about—what's the phrase?—sibling rivalry. Tony tells me he read it."

"So I heard."

We talk for a while—in fact at first the atmosphere's slightly edgy because of what we're *not* saying. Then I ask her, "Are you going to see Tony again?"

She shakes her head firmly. "Things are just beginning to uncomplicate themselves. And I wouldn't be able to do that to Vicky. I wouldn't have let any of what happened happen if I'd known about her in the first place."

"But you'd still like to see him?"

She nods, then shrugs.

"Do you love him?"

"I don't know. I thought I did. A few days ago." She leans toward me, smiling, but her eyes are sort of heavy and sad. "I'm leaving first thing tomorrow, Nick. I wanted to see you before."

It takes me a while to digest this. "Where are you going?" I ask.

"To my mother's for a while. Then to Florida for three weeks, if my dad will cough up the airfare."

"Even though you can't stand the floozie?"

She smiles. "If you can live with Tony, I'll make an effort with her." She pauses, leans back in her chair. "I *could* have stayed here—I still have the option—but I'm confused and unclear, and I still feel like I'm the cause of this trouble. If I hadn't been here—"

"You should stop thinking that way," I protest. "You just got caught in an ugly scene. Without you perhaps it would've gone on and on, growing worse."

"Will you write to me?" she goes, opening the copy of *Deuce*, which has her signature, address, and home number on the title page. "I'd like for us to keep in touch, if *you'd* like."

"Sure. Why not?"

She's smiling, but she sounds slightly cool. "You'll need time to sort yourself out. Me too. It hasn't been the easiest vacation I've ever had. Certainly the weirdest. Think I need a vacation to recover from it." Before she leaves, she leans over to kiss me, first on both cheeks, then on the lips. She smells of fresh-scented soap and talc, and I think of the moment in Ferdinand's when she slapped my cheek and feel pleased to know we're still friends. "Take care," she says.

"You too," I go, watching her depart the ward. Just before she's out of sight, she turns and blows me a kiss, and I lift up my good arm and clench my fingers, pretending to catch it.

In the late afternoon Tony turns up with Vicky, bringing chocolates and a get-well card from the school that almost everyone in the class has signed or scrawled over; even Rees has scribbled his name, the phony. There's a picture of Garfield with a bandaged leg on the front. And for a time I lie there reading all the names over and over, thinking: They *care*! I never imagined they even *thought* about me. Although, I have to admit, Bob Clark and Terry Mulligan haven't bothered to show their faces.

So Tony flops on the foot of the bed and Vicky drags up a chair and touches her hand to my forehead and smiles.

"You're looking good, Nick," she says.

"You too," I reply. She really does.

It was Vicky who called for the cops that day from a public phone outside the school grounds. Alex had approached her in the yard after I ran toward town, and between them they sort of talked things out and eventually put two and two together. Alex, confused and tearful, described everything Tony and I had put her through since the night she'd found herself locked in the basement of that house, from the role-playing game Tony sprang on her to the time when I broke down and confessed in the coffee shop. We really must have hurt her, when you think about it. They were still puzzling over what it all meant and what might have happened to Tony when Bob Clark showed up, desperate to find me because he needed the house key that I'd borrowed. His old man and the contracting team he works with were due to move in and finish the basement, and Bob needed the key, he said, before the old man got wise. If he ever found out about the parties, Bob would be dog meat. He'd no sooner mentioned this than Alex and Vicky sort of looked at each other, horrified. That was when they knew.

"What you did," Vicky tells me now. "It was terrible, Nick, really terrible. Almost unforgivable."

"I know. I agree."

"You had everyone worried, you know."

"Me too. Let's just say I've been ill for a while and now I have a chance to put things right." I hand the card back to her, and she places it beside the others on my night table. There are many cards, from many people I thought never thought of me. "It helps to know how many people care—even though they know what I've done. I never thought anyone would ever forgive me for that."

She nods, takes my left hand gently—it's bruised purple and brown and very tender—in hers. "Maybe sometimes other people can surprise you," she says, and flashes a glance toward Tony. "They'll forgive you if they really understand. Remember that guy who blew a hole in the Leonardo cartoon with a shotgun? Walked right inside the National Gallery, picked his moment, pulled out the weapon, and *pow*! People forgave him because he was crying out for help—for someone to take notice of him. Maybe, in a way, that's what you were doing too. Crying help."

"At Tony's expense."

"Yes, well," Tony says coyly. "But nobody's innocent—neither of us is. We both went too far. We were both out of line. But now we have to learn to put up with each other. We have to—"

"Talk to each other," I interject. "Alex said that was our problem, and it is. It has been. We always brooded over our differences instead of settling them, talking them out. Boys never talk, she said. We just fight."

"Right." Vicky smiles, broadly and warmly. "We girls are such superior beings, of course, we never need *telling* those things."

There's a lull before Tony takes over. "Something I just had to tell you," he says. "It's about what happened on the cliff walk all that time ago. When I pushed you in the ditch and ran ahead."

"That's funny," I tell him. "I've been thinking about that myself."

"You have?"

"Lately it's been hard to keep it off my mind. All these years I've hated your guts for cheating, because you wanted to get there first. Then it struck me it's a damn good thing you did."

"That's what I was about to tell you," he goes, with this look of astonishment. "The same thought struck me too. I kept thinking—sometimes even dreaming, having nightmares—about the edge of the cliff when I ran toward it, just at that point where the barrier was broken.

And Jesus, I had to pull up so sharply to stop myself going over. I even caught a glimpse of the rocks and sea down below before I managed to stop. I could've been dead right there and then." Then he looks at me sort of questioningly. "Is that what you were thinking too?"

"Yes. And after a while it struck me: If I'd done what you did—pushed you aside and rushed ahead—I *would've* been dead on the rocks. No question. I wouldn't have been able to pull up, because—"

"Because you were faster," he says. "You were always like lightning." We stare at each other for perhaps a full minute, agog. "And so I pushed you aside because I always resented your being better than me. I admired you for it, watching you race, but I always wished I had the same talent. I could never make first place like you. I had to play dirty to get what I wanted."

"In our different ways we both played dirty, I guess," I say.

"In our different ways we're both very much alike," Tony says.

"That's what I hate. I want to be different. I don't want to be anything like you."

"Nor me like you."

We all laugh.

Later he tells me he's taking up the guitar again. He hasn't been involved in music since we moved to Milton Green High. There are two kids who're trying to form a band called Distortion, but they still need a drummer to make up the foursome. "Perhaps you could give it a go," Tony says. "You'll need a way to burn off that excess energy if you're not going to be running for six months."

"Who needs a drummer with a busted elbow?"

"Ah," he goes. "That could be a problem."

"Thanks for the idea, though." You can tell he's been giving it some thought.

After they've gone, I just sort of lie there listening to the old guy in the next bed complain to the nurses—you're all out to get me, the food here is awful—and eventually I'm able to tune him out and think about everyone out there who cares. I think about Tony—for the first time in years without gritting my teeth. And I think about Alex, and in my head I compose the first few lines of a letter. Later still, I begin to read *Deuce*, the book Alex brought me, at first rather slowly—it's a long time since I've read, and I have to reread several sentences over to catch the full meaning—but after a while I find myself lost inside it, anxious to know what happens next, reading until I fall asleep and start dreaming.

It's a story about these two brothers.